At the Edge of the World

KARI JONES

At the Edge of the World

ORCA BOOK PUBLISHERS

Library and Archives Canada Cataloguing in Publication

Jones, Kari, 1966–, author
At the edge of the world / Kari Jones.

Issued in print and electronic formats.
ISBN 978-1-4598-1062-4 (paperback).—ISBN 978-1-4598-1063-1 (pdf).—
ISBN 978-1-4598-1064-8 (epub)

I. Title.
PS8619.05328A82 2016   JC813'.6   C2016-900538-0
                      C2016-900539-9

First published in the United States, 2016
Library of Congress Control Number: 2016933646

Summary: In this novel for teen readers, best friends Maddie and Ivan
struggle to cope with Ivan's father's alcoholism.

*Orca Book Publishers is dedicated to preserving the environment and has
printed this book on Forest Stewardship Council® certified paper.*

Orca Book Publishers gratefully acknowledges the support for its publishing
programs provided by the following agencies: the Government of Canada through
the Canada Book Fund and the Canada Council for the Arts, and the Province of British
Columbia through the BC Arts Council and the Book Publishing Tax Credit.

Cover design by Rachel Page
Front cover images by Creative Market and iStock.com
Back cover images by Creative Market

ORCA BOOK PUBLISHERS
www.orcabook.com

Printed and bound in Canada.

19 18 17 16 • 4 3 2 1

To the Wildwood Writers, for all the years together.

ONE

Ivan

Des is drunk again. It's not supposed to be this way. It's meant to be me, the teenage son, who gets drunk and acts stupid, and Des, the father, who takes care of me. But that's not how it is. I'm the sober one. He's the one puking into the flower bed.

We tussle over the van key. "No way," I say, prying his fingers apart. Across the road in the school parking lot, someone laughs and a car engine starts. More people come out of the auditorium. Still two weeks left of school, but that never stopped anyone in Bear Harbour from calling it end of term and throwing a party.

"I'm fine," Des says. Even drunk he's stronger than I am. He snaps his fingers shut around the key.

"Get in the van," he orders. He lunges at me, and I stumble and fall. My feet land under the rear wheel, my head in the flower bed.

He nudges my side with his boot. "Ivan, get up."

I don't move; my head is throbbing. He stands over me, then lurches to the van door and yanks it open. A few seconds later he revs the engine.

I leap to my feet as he backs the van out over the spot I was lying in a second ago.

"Holy shit. You almost ran me over," I shout at him.

"But I didn't."

"You could have."

"Nah. I knew you'd get out of the way." He revs the engine again. "Get in," he says.

"Fuck you."

He turns his bleary eyes to me. "Fine then. You want to drive?"

I nod and hold my hand out, palm up. He turns off the ignition, pulls out the key and plops it into my hand. I shove the key in my pocket and walk away.

"Hey," he shouts.

I keep walking. The van door opens. There's silence for a second, then the door closes again. I don't turn around.

I stand in the drizzle at the edge of the Legion parking lot, listening to people laughing as they come and go. There's no movement from the van. A few more minutes and he'll be snoring. Trees creak around me. Surf booms. There's the scent of some spring flower.

When the parking lot is finally empty, I go back and peer in the window of the van. As I expected, he's snoring away in the driver's seat. It's not easy to shove a man his size out of the way, so after a couple of tries I give up and perch on his lap. I can reach the pedals at least, and the roads along our side of the bay are empty anyway. When I rev the engine to get the starter to catch, Des half wakes up and tries to push me off. "You're sitting on my leg," he says.

"Then get in the other seat," I say as I turn the van around to ease onto the road. Des groans as my leg pushes down on his so I can reach the pedal better, and he shuffles noisily over the gear shift to the passenger side.

"You sleep." If he sleeps, he won't try to take over the wheel or throw up all over me or try to open the door or any of the other stupid drunken things he's done in the past, so I hum him a lullaby for the few minutes it takes to drive out of town and up the hill to our house.

"Get up," I say when I turn the engine off.

Des grunts, half asleep, but it's raining hard now, and despite the shelter of the cedar trees overhanging the driveway, rain's leaking through the roof of the van. A patch of water is already spreading along his thigh.

"Up," I say again. I get out and go around the van to open his door. He slides right into me, and I steady him so he doesn't fall.

"It's raining," he says.

Genius.

"Shut the door," I say, and he shoves it with his shoulder.

It takes me a minute of fumbling with the lock before I can get the door to the house open. Des slumps against the wall, snoring. I have to shove him to get him inside.

"It's cold in here," Des says as he pulls off his jacket and lets it fall to the ground. He shuffles to the living room, and from the hallway I can hear the ring of metal as he bumps into the woodstove, and the tinkle of glass as he pulls a beer bottle from the case.

My clothes are damp from standing in the drizzle, so I head to the bathroom, where I strip and start a hot shower. The water feels great on my back and shoulders, and I want to stay until the water loses its heat, but I don't trust what Des is up to out there, so I cut it short.

"What are you doing?" I ask Des when I come back to the living room. There's smoke in the air, but it takes me a while to realize it's not coming from the woodstove—a lit cigarette is dangling from Des's fingers. He is asleep on the couch. Ash drops from the cigarette to the floor, where it smolders in the carpet. He sighs in his sleep, and the cigarette falls from his hand into the pile of ash. I watch the smoke curl up along Des's arm until the smell changes from cigarette burning to carpet burning, and then I step forward and stomp it out. I also pour half his bottle of beer on it, just to make sure. The packet of cigarettes is on the coffee table, so I grab it and the lighter. Then I check the woodstove but see that he hasn't lit it. On my way upstairs I lock the front door and turn off all the lights except the one leading up the stairs.

In my room, I toss the cigarettes into a corner, then climb into bed and lie still, listening to the sound of Des crying in his sleep while I wait for the covers to warm me up.

* * *

In the morning, Des is still snoring on the couch when I come downstairs. Shaking his shoulder doesn't wake him, and neither does shouting in his ear, so I leave him there, gather up the empties around him and pile them into the recycling, which needs to be put out today. There are bottles and cans all over the kitchen and living room, so by the time I've gathered them all, the bin is full and looks worth taking to the road.

There's just enough milk in the fridge for a bowl of cereal. I should have poured the milk before I took out the recycling. Instead, I put the carton next to the door to remind me we need more.

I spend the morning sawing wood. Our closest neighbors, Bo and Peter, have ordered some shelves for the front hallway of their house. I've been trying to get started on them for a while but have had problems figuring out how to make the shelves go around the corners. I think I've finally got a solution, so I put in my earbuds and bliss out to music and the whine of the saw for a while.

About lunchtime, Des tears out through the door. His eyes are tiny pebbles. His breath is dynamite.

"You should have woken me," he says. "I had a shift."

"Aw, shit, Des." The foreman at the mill gave him a final warning last week. One more unexplained absence and that's the end. He's only kept Des on for as long as he has for my sake. People feel sorry for me because Des and I have been alone since my mother walked out on us when I was eight. Ten years since she picked her cigarettes up from the table, said, "Excuse me, please," walked out the door and drove away.

"Will he pay you? Give you severance?"

He shakes his head.

He pulls up one of the metal bar stools we use as lawn chairs and sinks into it. I rev the saw and let it bite into the wood. Cedar chips spray between us, but my hands are shaking and the cut is wrong, so I throw the damaged piece of wood to the ground.

"Shit, Des," I say again.

He rubs his head with his hands and stares at me.

I work in silence, counting my breaths—one in, one out—to steady myself. I can't afford to waste any more wood.

"What are you making?" Des asks.

"Shelves for Bo and Peter's front hall." We've talked about it before, so he nods and says, "You figured out how to get them around the corner?"

"I think so."

"These your drawings?" He picks up the notebook lying near the steps to the house and studies my notes. "Yeah, this is good," he says, "but…" He takes my pencil and draws on the opposite page.

"Try this," he says.

His drawings are perfect. A brilliant answer for a tricky problem. I should have thought of it myself.

"Thanks," I say, though my voice is tight. I could have used this answer ages ago. Saved myself hours of figuring it out.

"No problem," he says. "What's a dad for?"

There is no answer to that question, so I straighten my goggles on my face and bend back to my work. The next time I look up, he's gone.

TWO

Maddie

"Did you get in?" Ivan asks. To avoid answering, I straighten my board and paddle hard to catch the wave. The green water swells around me, and I curve my board to its contours until it fades below me.

Somehow, Ivan's still right next to me. He lies down on his board and stares at me. "Come on, Maddie. Did you get into that university or not?"

"You've got cedar chips in your hair," I say.

He shakes his head, the only part of him not covered by his wet suit. "I spent the morning cutting wood," he says. "Got a good chunk of Bo's shelves done."

Ivan's made a lot of shelves for my dad Bo, and somehow there's always a need for more. Bo's a science writer who works from home, and Peter, my other dad, is a violin maker. He has a studio at the back of the house that he always wants more shelves for. Between them, they buy books like most people buy groceries. It makes for a very full house, but we like it that way.

"Did your dad help you?" I ask, because Ivan always says no one knows wood like Des does.

"Yeah," he says, though the way he turns his head from me makes me think there's more to that statement than he's letting on.

"Yeah, but…?" I ask.

He shrugs. His typical answer to a question he doesn't want to answer. Well, that's both of us not answering questions then.

"Let's catch this one," I say to cover the silence, and we both straighten our boards. When we ride, it's like we become only bodies. White water bursts around my head; smooth green water slips under the board. The roar blots out all other sounds. Salt stings my eyes and lands in my mouth, but I rise on the board, and I'm flying, so it doesn't matter. There's nothing but motion for a few seconds.

The wave dies down, and I can see Ivan close by, on another wave now. He bends and flows with the water. Ivan's clumsy sometimes, bangs himself up and is always covered in cuts and bruises, but he's been surfing since we were in kindergarten, maybe even before, and on water he's a seal. There's nothing I like more than playing at being a seal with Ivan, though today I try to keep a wave or two between us so I don't have to get into a discussion about going to Emily Carr University. I'll get enough of that on Monday at school. Everyone's making their plans for next year. Tension is high. Questions abound.

I shouldn't have applied, but it was part of a deal I made with Peter. He said I could live in the house for free for the summer as long as I applied to at least one major art school. But getting accepted doesn't mean I'm going.

We surf for an hour or so, until the tide's too low, and then we both ride a small wave to shore. We lounge in the shallows, neither of us willing to leave the waves quite yet, but the water's still really cold in these last days of May even with a wet suit, so soon I pull up my board and walk to the high-tide line, where I've left my towel and water bottle. Ivan follows.

"Unzip me?" I ask. My hands are too cold to do it myself. Ivan lays his board against a log and takes off his gloves. He pulls at his sleeves to drain them, then tugs at the zipper at the neck of my wet suit. It doesn't move.

"You got in, didn't you?" he asks again.

There's no point avoiding this conversation anymore. It's inevitable. "Emily Carr University of Art and Design. Yeah, I got in."

"Peter'll be happy." Ivan tries the zipper again. It often sticks when it's full of salty water.

"Yeah."

"You should go. You know that, right?"

"Seriously, why is everyone in such a rush to get rid of me?"

"Don't be an ass, Maddie. You know that's not what it is."

"Bo and Peter—especially Peter—think I have to go to university to blossom as an artist and become famous or something. Peter always tells me about how his life would have been easier if he'd had a chance to get a degree, how he wouldn't have had to spend all those years starving, and Bo goes on about how university was the best time of his life. Then they get into arguments about what I should study—straight-up painting or art history or whatever. It gets so tedious. They don't even listen to me. Honestly, Ivan, sometimes I envy you. Des doesn't care what you do. Must be nice."

I can hear Ivan's intake of breath at the back of my neck. He yanks hard, and the zipper finally comes loose.

"Sorry," I say.

"Whatever."

"No, seriously, I'm sorry."

"It's fine, Maddie. Now do me."

Ivan's wet suit is older than mine, and the zipper is even stickier. It's so crusted with salt, I have to pour some fresh water from my bottle over it to get it going.

I find a log to hide behind and struggle out of my wet suit and bathing suit and into dry clothes. Neither of us says anything. I shouldn't have said that about Des not caring. Des can be tough going sometimes. He drinks way too much, and there have been times when I wonder if Ivan ends up being the parent in the relationship. Plus, I don't like it when Ivan's upset with me. It unbalances my world.

Ivan reaches past me to drink from my water bottle before we head up the beach. "I'm starving," he says.

"I'll make you some lunch," I say, because I want him to feel better and because I suspect no one in his house ever goes grocery shopping. Two guys living alone—honestly, they live up to every stereotype.

"Thanks," he says with a huge smile.

We gather our boards and walk along the beach to my house. There's smoke coming out of the chimney.

As we walk, I tell Ivan about the series of paintings I'm working on. They're acrylic on easel-sized pieces of particle board left over from when we renovated the bathroom a couple of years ago. The series is about ravens, how smart they are, how they have a culture and a language. I'm trying to show in paint what I see every day outside my bedroom window.

As Ivan listens, he smiles and nods. I take his silence to mean he's in a better mood.

At the house we brush the sand off our bare feet and stack the surfboards in the rack. We take turns rinsing our wet suits under the outside tap, then hang them on pegs next to the surfboards. The perfect setup for a house on the beach.

"Remember when Des made these?" I ask Ivan, pointing at the rack and pegs.

"Sure, I helped him."

I'd forgotten that. He was a skinny kid, and he'd followed Des everywhere. He runs his hand over the wood. "Needs a touch-up."

I leave him examining the rack and go into the house to make lunch. I'm glad Ivan's here. I haven't told Peter yet that I got into Emily Carr, but I know he's going to ask at lunch. He asks every day. Maybe with Ivan here, he won't explode when I tell him I'm not going.

When I've got bread cut and bowls of chili laid out on the table, I call everyone in. Before they get there, I put a small bowl of strawberry flowers in the center of the table.

"Beautiful as always, Maddie," says Peter as he pulls his chair out and sits down. He's talking about the table, not me.

"Great news that Maddie got into Emily Carr, eh?" Ivan says.

Oh, Ivan! If looks could kill, I'd slice him in half from across the table. Peter and Bo both beam at me.

"I knew it!" Peter says.

"Well done, Maddie," says Bo.

I can't look at them when I say, "I'm not going to accept their offer."

No one responds. The silence drags until I'm forced to look up from my plate. All three of them are staring at me.

"What?" Peter says.

"I don't want to go."

"That wasn't our deal, Maddie," Peter says.

"I said I would apply. I never said I would go."

"That's not the spirit of the deal, and you know it."

Bo leans across the table and puts his hand over mine. "At least think about it for a few days, Maddie. Emily Carr is hard to get into. Many young artists would love to trade places with you."

"I've done nothing but think about it since I sent off the application. I don't want to go. I don't want to go to any university. Not yet. I just want to paint." They don't get it. They hear the words, but they don't understand the meaning. I can tell by the way they're all still staring at me.

"You can always defer, go later," Bo says.

They're already totally upset with me, so I might as well tell them the whole deal right now. "It's a one-time-only offer. At least, the scholarship is," I say.

"A scholarship!" Bo exclaims.

Peter shoves his chair away from the table and stands up. "I can't believe you, Maddie. Throwing away such an amazing opportunity. Well, I guess this means you'll have to start paying rent. No time like the present to experience the reality of being a starving artist." He throws his napkin on the table and storms out. Typical Peter, being so dramatic, but still, it's hard not to cry.

Bo lets go of my hand. "He spent a long time being hungry, Maddie. You have to expect him to overreact. He'll calm down. But Maddie, don't say no quite yet, okay?" He gathers our dishes and takes them into the kitchen. Ivan follows him, and I can hear Bo telling Ivan about meeting Sartre—the actual Sartre—when he was at university. Ivan laughs and says, "Okay, who's Sartre?"

I leave the table and go into the living room, where I settle in on the window seat. There's a sketchpad lying on the cushion. I keep it there so I can doodle or draw things I see from the window. The pad is a couple of years old, and the early drawings are mostly of whales, and they're mostly rough, but some of them are pretty good. The later ones are better. Stronger lines, more character. The sketchpad is open to a drawing of Bo sitting at his desk, and though it's hard to be objective about my own work, I like it. It captures the way he looks when he's thinking.

Ivan comes in from the kitchen and sits next to me on the window seat.

"That's awesome," he says, pointing to the drawing of Bo.

"Thanks."

"Do you think Peter's really going to charge you rent?"

I shrug. Peter and I have been arguing about this for months. He lived rough and hungry for a long time and thinks university is my ticket out of that life. But the one time I pointed out that even though he never went to university he makes a pretty good living as a violin maker, he went ballistic and even showed me a scar he has on his upper arm from the time he was living in a shed and tore it on a rusty nail. As if that has anything to do with anything. The only reason he got to be a violin maker was because of Bo's support, and he never forgets it.

I crave some time to explore on my own, to figure out what kind of art I want to do. I don't want people telling me what my strengths are just yet. I need to find out for myself. I'll live in a shed if I have to.

"I just wish Peter would realize I'm not him," I say to Ivan.

Ivan laughs. "You so are him."

"No I'm not."

"You're a mini-Peter. Stubborn and dramatic. Not hard to figure out who your bio dad is."

"What! I'm not stubborn," I say, but then Bo walks into the room.

"Storm's coming," he says. "Ivan, you'd best leave now before the winds get too wild."

Ivan reaches over and picks up my sketchbook and hands it to me. "Yeah. Des'll be wondering where I am." He smirks at me to show he doesn't mean what he says at all.

"I'll walk you," I say. I'm not really upset at Ivan for saying I'm just like Peter. I know it's true. That doesn't mean it's going to be any easier living with him while he gets used to the idea that I'm definitely not going to university in the fall.

The incoming storm has blurred the edges of the world, and we can't see clearly where the water ends and the land begins. We walk slowly, balancing on the logs, like neither of us wants to get where we're going.

When we reach the pathway that goes up to Ivan's house high on the hill, he stops to adjust his hold on his surfboard. "Good luck with Peter," he says.

"Yeah."

"It's just because he cares."

"Well, sometimes I wish he didn't care so much." As soon as I say it, I wish I hadn't.

Ivan snorts and says, "Be careful what you wish for," then spins on his heel and walks up the path.

I head down the beach for home. The wind tears at my hair and makes walking hard, but I don't care—it's exactly what I'm in the mood for. I'm in for a long fight with Peter on this one. I know it.

THREE

Ivan

Des and I stand at the window. Des's hands are still shaky from last night's drinking, and he squints at me like he's got a migraine. Our house is at the top of the hill, so there's always a good show in a windstorm like this, but tonight it makes me worry about Maddie and Bo and Peter down there right on the beach. Wind like this could whip up waves big enough to drag their house out to sea. Des has a crease down his forehead that only appears when he's worried.

"Do you think we should go down and check on them?" I ask.

"Who?" he says.

"Bo and Peter and Maddie," I say.

He chews his lip but doesn't seem to have heard me.

"Should we?" I ask.

"That house's seen worse storms than this," he says.

"I guess." He's right, but still. It's a bad one.

A zigzag of lightning streaks across the sky, getting bigger and bigger until it crashes, throwing flames up into the trees and way out into the bay.

"Holy shit." I jump back from the window, spilling coffee over my fingers.

"Looks like it hit something," Des says. We both peer out the window. At the far end of the beach, where it curves into the headland, there's fire, and already the smell of smoke wafts through the windows.

"That's Maddie's house," I say.

Des is already half out the door, so I run after him, ignoring my burned fingers and pulling on rain boots at the same time. Together we race across the grass at the back of the house and slither down the muddy path through the forest to the beach. Usually we can move fast on the beach, but tonight the tide's so high there's hardly any sand, just driftwood piled against the hillside. It slows us down, and we curse and shout as we stumble along. Waves crash over us and drag at our feet, so we have to climb back into the forest and run along the path.

It's hard to see. It smells like a building is burning. The stench of melting paint hits us, and we gag.

"Shit, that's awful," says Des.

I bite back the vomit that rises in my throat and carry on running, though it's hard to keep going toward the smell, and now the air stings, making it hard to breathe. I wish it was raining.

"Come on," says Des without looking back, and I stumble along behind him until we reach the far end of the bay, where we find Maddie.

"Thank God you're here," she says. "I wish we got good cell coverage down here. I'll have to run up to the road to call 9-1-1."

The air is clogged with smoke, but Maddie leads us around the house until we can see flames coming from one of the sheds. The fire sounds like a lot of people shouting.

"Where are Bo and Peter?" I shout to her above the noise of the fire and wind.

She points down the path. I can just make out Bo spraying water from a garden hose onto the burning shed. I turn to join them, but Maddie pulls on my arm and points to the house. She moves her mouth, and I can't hear what she's saying, but then Des, who's standing with us, nods and shouts, "Save the house."

He sweeps Maddie's hair back so he can shout into her ear. She listens, then says something to him and points before she leaves us and runs up the path to the road. Des and I pull our T-shirts up over our noses, then rush to the side of the house, where we find some more garden hoses tangled against the wall. We don't speak as we gather them in our arms. The only outside tap is already being used, so I shove open the kitchen door and wrestle the hose into the sink, but the tap's not meant to have a hose attached to it, and no matter how much I fumble with it, I can't join them together.

"Laundry room," Des shouts through the window.

I should have thought of that. The washing sink is in the back hallway next to the kitchen, and it doesn't take too long to screw in the hose. When I catch up with him, Des is already running around the outside of the house with it, spraying water everywhere.

"Douse everything you can see, including the roof," he shouts, handing me the hose. It's hot even with the water gushing everywhere, it's getting harder to breathe, and somehow it's getting louder too.

"Spray me," Des shouts, so I turn the hose on him and he ducks and twists until he's soaked, and then he pushes deeper into the smoke to a small garden shed. A moment later he returns with a hatchet in his hand, which he swings into one of the saplings Bo planted last year as a windbreak between the path to the sheds and the house. The tree falls on the first swing, and we both watch it land.

"I could have soaked that," I say.

"We need a firebreak." He swings the hatchet against the second tree, and I know he's right—the trees make a pathway for the fire right to the house. The two trees closest to the sheds are already in flames, and the third one is smoking.

"Peter and Bo are still next to the shed, fighting the fire. They're going to get caught," Des says. He hands me the hatchet. "Keep cutting until you can't breathe, then get out of here."

"Where are you going?" I ask.

He takes the hose from my hands and showers himself with water again before he says, "Peter and Bo will be trapped. Soon." He turns the hose on me, and the shock of cold water slaps me in the face and chest.

"If you have trouble breathing, get to the beach."

"Where's Maddie?" I haven't seen her since we got here.

"She's up at the road, waiting for the firefighters."

We both grimace, because it's clear no fire truck will be able to get anywhere near here. Des hands me back the hose and moves into the smoke, and I don't know whether to keep spraying water or cut down the trees. It seems like either will be pointless, but maybe I can at least clear a path for Bo and Peter and Des to come out of the smoke, so I point the hose down the path after Des and hope the water will clear the air.

I'm still aiming water down the path when Maddie appears from around the house with three firefighters. When they reach me, the three men huddle together and Maddie takes my arm. The two of us watch the firefighters wave their arms around as they make a plan. A minute later they break their huddle.

"You two get to the beach," one of them says. The ax in his hand is much bigger than mine.

"What about Bo and Peter?" Maddie asks. Her hair flies so thickly around her face, we can hardly hear her words.

"We'll worry about them," he says, but there's no need, because Bo and Peter and Des all come up the path at that moment.

"It's spread to the trees," Bo says. His voice is rough from smoke, and all three of them are coughing.

"Get to the beach—you've had too much smoke," says the firefighter, and before any of us can say anything he pulls a mask over his face and turns his attention to the remaining saplings.

"Come on," Des says, and he herds us down toward the ocean. It's only when we hit the fresh air of the beach that I realize how much my eyes sting and my throat hurts.

"I'm soaked," I say.

"We all are," Bo says. And then there's nothing more to say, so we just huddle in a row on a log that's high enough on the beach to avoid the waves but is not out of the wind.

It feels like forever until one of the firefighters comes back.

"It's not as bad as it could have been," he says. "Shed's gone though. And we had to cut down those saplings."

Peter nods.

"You guys need to get dry and drink some water," the firefighter says.

I stand up to start home, but I'm so cold my feet barely move, and I sit back down.

Maddie pulls my arm until I'm standing again.

"We'll keep at it a while longer. You lot get into the house. You look like shit," the firefighter says, pointing at me. "Get him inside and warm."

I'm about to protest, but Maddie takes my hand and leads me toward her house, and I decide I do need to get warm and dry. As fast as possible.

For a while, Maddie and I are alone in the house, and it seems like I should say something reassuring, but the stench from the fire is in my nostrils and on my hair and my clothes, and the only thing I can think about is getting rid of it. Maddie doesn't even wait for me to ask before she hands me a towel and a pair of Peter's sweatpants and points to the shower.

"You stink," she says.

The water feels good, and I stay in the shower a long time. When I come out, I find Maddie and Bo and Peter and Des in the kitchen. Maddie hands me a glass of water, which I down in two gulps, and then another, which I drink more slowly, and finally a cup of hot chocolate, and we all go sit in the living room. The waves are higher than I've ever seen them; a couple break over the front deck, sending Maddie and me leaping out of the window seat. It's raining now, which is good, but it's too loud to talk.

Maddie and I sit there watching the storm while the others shower. I'm so tired it's hard to keep my eyes open, and maybe I even fall asleep, because one second I'm sitting there next to Maddie, and the next she's got her head on my shoulder and we're all wrapped up in a blanket.

Des comes in from the bathroom with a bundle of wet clothes under his arm and says, "We should get home, buddy. Let these guys get some sleep."

"Yeah." I start to unravel myself from the blanket and from Maddie. She whimpers when I move her head off my shoulder, so I'm extra gentle when I settle her into the corner of the window seat. Everyone whispers so we won't wake her as Des and I leave.

"Thanks, guys. I don't even want to think about losing this house." Peter's voice shakes a bit as he speaks.

Bo nods. "Yeah. Thanks so much."

"We're here for you, buddy. You can count on us," Des says.

My stomach twists a little when Des says that. It's true— Des is always there for them when they need him. He's good in an emergency, and he knows how to put on a good front. A very good front. That's one thing he knows how to do.

FOUR

Maddie

It's morning when a pain in my neck wakes me. I'm shoved into the corner of the window seat, and it takes a couple of seconds to free myself from the blankets that have become tangled around me.

The whole house stinks of smoke and something else I can't put my finger on, which makes the back of my throat tickle unpleasantly. Burnt things.

I head into the kitchen for a glass of water. Peter is standing over the stove, cooking up a mess of scrambled eggs, and Bo is sitting at the table, looking shattered.

"Bo, are you okay?" I ask. Bo's my rock. He's everyone's rock. Seeing him like this makes my stomach clench.

"I think some food will help," Peter answers from the stove. Bo puts out his arms, and I go ahead and sit on his lap like a little kid.

"Oof," he says.

"Oh, thanks," I say. It's a joke between us, since Bo is one of the biggest men I've ever seen, and he can still carry me in his arms if he feels like it. Luckily for me, I have Peter's more delicate genes, not Bo's.

He squeezes me tightly, and I can also feel Peter stroking my hair, so we're all touching, like one big person, all soaking each other up. For a tiny second I'm glad the shed caught fire and brought us all together. I used to feel like my two dads had their arms around me and each other all day every day, like no matter what people or life threw at us, it wouldn't matter at all. I haven't felt that way lately. Stupid university.

Peter returns to his eggs, and when they're ready, I get up to pull out the cutlery and some plates. Bo stands and stretches, then sits back down, but this time he sits straighter.

"You okay?" I ask when I bend over him to place the cutlery on the table.

He nods. "I wore myself out, that's all."

I'm sure that's not all. I'm sure training a hose on a fire that's blossoming and growing around you takes its toll. But I just smile at him.

"Sit next to me," he says, so I do.

Bo's silent throughout the meal, which means no one talks, because he's the one in the family that keeps conversation going. I don't care, though, because the longer we sit here together, my little family, the more right the world feels.

"What was in the shed?" Peter asks once his plate is empty.

Bo looks away from him as he says, "Mostly wood."

Peter freezes, and I do too.

"Wood? As in *my* wood?" Peter asks.

Bo nods.

"My wood that I've been drying?"

"I'm sorry, Peter, I know you asked me to move it ages ago. I just didn't get around to it yet."

Peter doesn't say anything, but his whole body slumps. The wood that's just burned is worth thousands and thousands of dollars. I exhale slowly. I'm afraid to look at either of them.

Peter glares at Bo. "The ebony?" he asks.

Bo nods.

Without saying anything, Peter shoves his plate away, gets up and leaves the room. Bo and I don't look at each other, and we don't say anything.

We both know how important that wood was.

*   *   *

Peter's gone for most of the day. Before he leaves, I overhear him talking to Bo, and though I can't hear all of what they're saying, I do catch the words *Maddie* and *university*. Peter was planning to sell a violin to help pay the cost of my tuition. Now he won't be able to.

It's Sunday, so I get the last of my homework done, then spend the rest of the day in my room, trying to concentrate on painting. Trying, but there are a lot of thoughts swirling around in my brain, and I end up doodling in my sketchbook instead. Having the wood burn should make things easier for me, because I don't have the money to pay for the tuition not covered by the scholarship myself. No violin, no tuition—an easy way out. Somehow it doesn't feel that way.

From my bedroom window at the back of the house, I can see Bo poking around where the shed used to be, and I know he's looking for anything he can salvage. He must be feeling pretty bad today.

It's late when Peter comes home. He comes straight to my room and knocks on my door.

"Come in."

Peter is tall and ruddy, and his thick hair makes him look healthy. But not today. He looks gray, and his shoulders are stooped. He sits on the end of the bed and flips through my sketchbook.

"Some of the wood's okay. I think I can salvage enough of the ebony."

"I'm glad, Peter."

"Emily Carr. I'm so proud of you, Maddie."

The doodles stare up at me. I want to tell him again, *I'm not going, Peter. I don't want to go.* But I can't find the courage. Not when he's sitting on the end of my bed looking like he's aged ten years in a day.

"I know you can't see it now, Maddie, but you really must go. It'll change the world for you, and you can't even imagine how much you're going to learn."

"Peter…"

"Maddie, it'll be the best time of your life. Don't deny yourself that. Give it some more thought. Promise?" He pushes the sketchbook toward me and stands up.

"I've done nothing but think about it, Peter."

"What have you got against going to university?"

"Nothing. I'll probably end up going."

"Good." Peter smiles.

"No, Peter. You're not listening to me. I meant I'll probably end up going sometime later."

"You've been accepted now, Maddie. You've already told us that offer's not going to be there later. This might be your only opportunity to go."

"That's a chance I'll have to take."

Peter glowers at me, and it's hard to meet his eyes. "Five, ten years from now, Bo and I might not be able to help you with tuition, you know."

I nod.

"So you're just going to throw this scholarship away?"

"That's not how I see it. I want to see the paintings in the Louvre, and in the Picasso museum in Barcelona, and in the National Museum in Sweden. Travel, you know."

"Must be nice. How are you planning to pay for all this travel?"

"I don't know. I'll find a way."

Peter shakes his head. "Being a hungry artist is tough, Maddie."

"I'm okay with that."

Peter blows air through his mouth, but it doesn't come out as a word. He walks out of the room, and a few seconds later I see him through the bedroom window. He's chopping firewood, fast and hard, though it's too late in the season to need wood.

My doodles stare up at me until I take my pencil and scribble all over the page.

FIVE

Ivan

Des wakes me up a couple of days after the fire by pulling the sheets off my bed. "Jesus, Ivan, you going to sleep all day?" he asks.

I pull my pillow over my head and try to recapture the dream I was having. It's true that I haven't done much over the past couple of days, even though I should have been going to school for study sessions and getting ready for finals, but I'm still tired from our night of firefighting.

Des pulls the pillow off. "Come on. Arne says we can take out his boat."

"What for?"

"Bo says the storm the other night washed up some good wood."

"Why now?"

"The tide's good."

"I should study."

"When are your exams?"

"Next week."

"Plenty of time." He throws me a pair of jeans and says, "Hurry."

I fumble my way into my jeans and shoes and follow him to the van.

"How's your throat?" he asks as we climb in and he jiggles the ignition to get the engine started.

"Still rough. Yours?"

"Yeah, same," he says. "It'll take a while, I think. Smoke inhalation's bad for you."

"Yeah. It's a nice excuse for doing nothing for a couple of days," I say.

"What's that supposed to mean?"

"You could've been looking for a new job," I say.

Des snorts and says, "I'm not the only one."

"Like it's my responsibility to keep food on the table. I have exams, remember?"

We pull into the dock. I'm already set to bail on the day and head home. To hell with spending the day with Des. But when we get there, my friend Noah comes up to the van door.

"I asked Noah to join us," says Des as he turns off the ignition, and before he opens the van door and gets out, he leans over the gearshift and says, "I've got something worked out, for your information."

"A job?"

"You could call it that," he says.

"That's great. How come you didn't tell me?"

But Des has already jumped out of the van.

We head down the ramp and onto the dock, and then Noah and I settle ourselves on the bow of Arne's boat. Noah's new to Bear Harbour. He still thinks heading out to the islands to salvage driftwood is exciting. Despite my grumbling, I like being on the water. We've collected firewood from the islands ever since I can remember. When I was little, Mom used to wrap her arms around me to keep me warm, and it was my job to watch out for things floating in the water: logs, crab traps, Styrofoam—once, a dead sea otter. Des would pretend he hadn't seen it until I yelled to him it was there, and then he'd change his course dramatically, making both Mom and me squeal. Yeah, that's how things were before she left. Anyway, that's how I remember it.

Now, as we pull away from the dock, Noah tells me about this wave he caught yesterday. He's getting pretty good at surfing.

After a while Des heads the boat toward Pitbull Island. Crossing the channel is choppy, so Noah and I pull up our hoods and huddle, backs to the wind, until we round the headland of the island. The wide beach is filled with driftwood. As Des noses the boat onto shore, I pull a chain saw out of a toolbox in the cab of the boat and hoist it onto my shoulder. We all wade to shore and start hunting for good firewood.

"It has to be new. The old stuff has too much salt in it," says Des.

"Yeah, I know," I say.

"I was talking to Noah."

Bo was right. There are logs everywhere. "Looks like a lumberyard lost a boatload," says Noah.

"A barge overturned. Lost half a million dollars' worth of logs. Storm washed them all to shore," says Des.

"So this is salvage? Don't you need a license for that?" Noah asks, but neither Des nor I answer him.

It doesn't take long before I find a log long enough to be a telephone pole lying at the top of a big pile. I rev the saw, and a flock of small birds flies away.

"Sit on this, will you?" I ask Noah. He straddles the log to steady it as the saw bites into the grain. As the cut falls to the ground, Noah says, "Do you do this all the time?"

"Sure. I was about four the first time I came out with Des," I say.

"Seriously?"

"I was in charge of protecting the crabs. I had a little circle of stones, and every time someone found a crab under a log, they'd shout and I'd come to the rescue."

"It seems like it wouldn't be legal, taking all this wood," he says.

"It's only illegal if you sell the wood."

"My mom wasn't sure I should come."

I stand up and stretch my hand. The saw's heavy, and I need to take a break. My arm's still not as strong as it was before I broke it a couple of years ago.

"Want me to take a turn?" asks Noah.

I shake my head and say, "How come you came then?"

Noah uses his feet to push the log up and down like a teeter-totter. It's balanced perfectly in the middle.

"Sit on the other end," he says, so I clamber to the far end of the log. We're about the same size, Noah and me, both fairly tall and of medium build, though he's dark and I'm blond. We balance each other well.

For a few minutes we ride the log, taking turns swinging high into the air, then pushing off the ground. It's like being a kid again. But then Des shouts at us to quit messing around, and we go back to cutting the log into lengths. I cut and Noah hauls the lengths to the beach.

After about half an hour, I stand again and stretch. My arm is sore.

Noah says, "In answer to your question, I came because I'm okay with a little bit illegal."

"It wouldn't be you who got in trouble anyway," I say. "I mean, if there was any trouble to get into."

"Exactly," he says.

An hour later the boat is so full the words on the side of the hull are half in the water, and both of my arms ache from loading what we've cut on board.

"That's enough," says Des. "We'd better get going." The tide's still coming in, and the beach is a lot smaller than it was. Des unties the boat from the tree he threw the rope over, and we all push the bow, then hop in.

Noah seems relaxed. He doesn't say much, but he has a smile on his face. The two of us sit on the bow and share a bottle of water, then spread out across the deck to enjoy the sun. The water's calm between the islands, and the sun's warm on my face, and it doesn't take long before the sound of the engine lulls me almost to sleep.

I don't pay much attention when Des changes course—there are many ways back to Bear Harbour from the islands—but I sit up when we slow around a point and the bow is slapped by choppy waves. Des turns in to a small bay and cuts the engine, letting the boat drift. In front of us is a rickety wooden dock with a boat pulled up beside it and an orange buoy hanging off a tree at the beach end.

"What're we doing here?" I ask.

"I told Pedro I'd stop in on him," says Des. "I'll be quick." He steers the boat up to the dock. It's usually my job to hop out and cinch the line around the cleat, but that would mean I'm agreeing to stop here.

Fuck that. Pedro's an asshole.

I lie back down on the bow.

"Suit yourself. Noah, will you tie the rope?" Des asks.

Noah raises his eyebrows at me but hops off the boat and leans on the rope to pull the boat into place. His foot slips, and he staggers, and I have to leap from my spot and grab the end of the rope, pull with him and cinch it off.

"Thanks," says Noah, rubbing his hands.

I almost get back onto the boat, but it seems cruel to leave Noah with Des and Pedro, so instead I follow the two of them into the woods. A hundred feet along, the trail opens into a rocky clearing overlooking a crescent-shaped bay. A cedar-shingle house and some sheds huddle between the forest and the rocky shore. Laundry hangs on a line, and there's smoke coming out of a small chimney. It looks homey. Great camouflage.

Pedro comes to the door and calls out, "Hey. You brought the family. I thought you were coming alone."

Des grins. "Pedro! You know Ivan, and this is Noah, a new friend from Bear Harbour."

The old man looks Noah up and down, then wipes his hand on his pants and sticks it out. "Nice to meet you," he says.

Noah shakes his hand.

"Come on in," says Pedro, but I'm already walking down to the beach. "Got brownies," he calls after me.

I give him the finger and keep walking.

Noah follows me down to the beach, but as we pick our way among the logs to the sand, he says, "What was that about?"

Before I can reply, Pedro's little five-year-old grand-daughter, Willow, runs up the beach and launches herself at me. I stagger as I catch her in my arms and lift her over my shoulder. "Hi, Willow."

"Come look," she says, and she wiggles down and runs along the beach to a pile of rocks. I squat next to her. "What've you got there?"

"I'm making a home for these." She lifts one rock, and a purple shore crab skitters away.

"We'll help," I say. "How big should the rocks be?"

"That one." She points to a rock the size of a motorcycle.

"We can't lift that, you goose."

She shrugs her shoulders. "Okay, then, like this." She makes a double fist and holds it up.

Noah and I wander along the beach looking for rocks that might make a good home for sea crabs. When we reach the far end, Noah asks again, "What was that about with Pedro?"

I balance one rock on top of another before I reply. "He and I don't really get along."

"No shit. How come?"

"When Pedro and Des are together there's always some scheme going on, and it usually doesn't end well."

"What do you mean?"

"He has a way of arranging things so that it's never him who gets into trouble when things go wrong."

I don't think that's the kind of answer Noah's looking for, but it's what he's getting for now, because Willow catches up with us and holds out her hands. She's got a purple sea star spread across her palms.

"Wow, look at that," says Noah.

"Do you want to hold it?" Willow asks, and when Noah nods, she goes through a complicated procedure of passing it from her hands to his. He holds it up so he can look under it.

"That's sick," he says.

"No it's not—it's very healthy," says Willow, and both Noah and I laugh. We help her return the sea star to the water and let her show us the rest of the things she's found on the beach: limpets, winkles, clams, different kinds of coral. She points to each of them and makes Noah repeat their names.

When Des calls from the house, I say, "Bye, buddy. Until next time."

"Bye, Ivan," she says, and she throws her arms around me in that amazing way little kids have of hugging with their whole bodies, then runs back down the beach to her crabs. Noah follows me up the path to the house. There are two huge backpacks leaning against the front of the house now. Des hoists one over his shoulder and points to the other. "Bring that," he says to me.

"What is it?"

"Pedro's laundry," Des says, though the clothesline filled with shirts and socks is right behind me.

"Big stuff I need the dry cleaner to do for me. They said they can pick it up at your house," Pedro says, and though I still don't believe him, I hoist the backpack onto my shoulder and take it down to the dock.

We climb into the boat and settle the backpacks under a tarp. Des makes certain the packs are well covered before he starts the engine. Noah and I take our places on the bow. The sun is high now and feels great on my face as I lean back and let it lull me to sleep.

My friend Jack and his dad, Arne, are on the dock to meet us at Bear Harbour. Arne's our local RCMP officer, which is why he has such a nice boat. He's also a generous man. Which is why he lends it to us.

"I see you found some wood," says Arne when Des kills the engine.

"Sure did," says Des.

"I assume you're not going to sell this, Des," Arne says.

"Of course not." Des grins at Arne, who shakes his head but smiles back.

Noah and Des step off the boat, and Des says, "I'll go get the van."

"We can help you unload," Arne says, but Des says, "Nah, I got two strong boys here."

Arne laughs and says, "It's no problem. What are friends for?"

"Seriously, Arne, there are three of us," Des says. He hops onto the boat and leans into the cab. A minute later he backs out with a pack in each hand. He hands me one. "Take this," he says.

My arms are already filled with wood, but he glances at Arne and whispers, "Take it."

I drop the wood onto the pile and take the pack from him, and I force the scowl on my face into a smile as I pass Arne on my way off the boat.

"I'll see if there's a wheelbarrow free," I say. Des and I walk up the dock, each with a backpack on our shoulder.

"What's in here?" I ask.

"Not now. Let's get the wood into the van first" is all the answer I get. Shit, I knew Des would be up to something.

*   *   *

As soon as Des and I drop Noah off at his house, I scramble to the back of the van and rip open the lid of one of the backpacks. There's laundry there, all right, but it's hard to mask the smell of weed, even with plastic bags, and under a thin layer of towels my hands find what they're looking for.

"Holy shit, Des, how much is there?"

"Enough," he says.

"Enough for you to get busted for trafficking," I say.

"Enough to pay off some debts and get me going again while I wait to get paid." He turns to face me. "I'm getting a job. A real one," he says.

"Selling weed doesn't count as a job," I say, my voice trembling.

Des shifts in his seat so he's looking out the side window. His knuckles are white on the steering wheel. "I meant, I'm looking. I'm starting fresh. Turning over a new leaf. This thing with Pedro is a one-time deal. He knows that."

"Selling weed isn't turning over a new leaf. It isn't starting fresh. It's just digging a bigger hole than you're already in," I say.

"Jesus Christ, Ivan, nothing I do is ever good enough for you. I'm trying. Did you even notice I haven't had a drink since before the storm?" Des pulls up under the trees in our driveway and stops the van. He yanks open the door and stomps into the house. I clench and unclench my hands to stop myself from using them to punch his face.

By the time I've taken the firewood out of the van and stacked it beside the house, I'm breathing normally, but he's already three beers down. So much for not drinking. There's also already someone knocking at the door.

"You Des?" the guy asks when I open the door. I shake my head and point to the kitchen. The man disappears into the room, and a few seconds later Des comes out and heads to the van, where he pulls out one of the backpacks. I don't wait to watch the transaction. Instead, I head into town to look for Maddie.

SIX

Maddie

"What are you doing?" Peter asks me a couple of days after the fire.

"Studying."

"Why?"

"You know, exams. Grade twelve. Important." I wave my hand over the pile of papers in front of me.

Peter takes a mug from the shelf and pours himself a cup of coffee. "I mean, why bother if you're not going to university anyway?" He slams the mug onto the table like a challenge.

"Fine." I gather my notes into a pile.

"No, Maddie, don't be silly—keep studying."

"No. You're totally right. Why study? I'm just an igno-ramus who's not going anywhere in life."

"That's not what I mean, Maddie."

"Sure it is."

"Then you're calling me an ignoramus too," he says.

"Exactly. We'll be ignoramuses together."

He doesn't even look at me as he rushes out of the room.

* * *

Bo finds me sobbing on the beach. It's not very warm out, and I've wrapped my long cotton skirt around myself like a cocoon to keep warm.

"How come he has to be so mean?" I ask, wiping my eyes.

"Peter?"

I nod.

Bo sits down next to me and gathers a fistful of sand and rocks, which he lets trickle through his fingers. "He's not being mean, he's being scared."

"Of what?"

"That you're making your life harder than it has to be. Don't underestimate how hard Peter had it when he was young."

"But that was him, not me."

"I know. But he loves you, and he doesn't want the same thing to happen to you."

"What about you? Do you think I should go to Emily Carr?"

Bo gathers another fistful of the beach. For a minute he looks out at the water, and I think he's not going to answer, but then he says, "I don't think you should go unless you want to. No one wants to teach students who don't want to be there."

"That's something you learned when you were teaching?"

"Yep."

"So what do you think I should do?"

"That's up to you, Maddie, but if you aren't going to university, and you want to spend some time traveling, you need to think about how you're going to make that happen."

"Yeah, I know."

Bo pulls off his sweater and hands it to me. I pull it over my shoulders thankfully. Cotton skirts don't add a lot of warmth.

"Remember last year at the Salmon Festival you and Katia did those henna tattoos? I bet you could make some good change if you set up a stall at the market this summer," Bo says.

"You've been thinking about this," I say.

He shrugs and nods.

"It's brilliant. What a great idea. Thank you so much, Bo. It's awesome, really."

He laughs. "It's not that wonderful an idea. You're still going to have to find a proper job at some point."

"No, it's perfect. I loved making those tattoos." I stand up and pull off Bo's enormous sweater and hand it back to him. "I'm going to ask Katia right now if she still has any of those henna tubes. And I can look online for designs." My skirt is a bit damp where I've been sitting on it, but I don't care. "Thanks, Bo!" I almost run across the beach to the path. I'm heading up to the road to text Katia right now.

* * *

I set up my market stall on Saturday. It's not as polished as some of the setups around me, but considering I pulled it off super quickly, I'm pretty proud of it. I should make some good money this summer drawing henna tattoos for tourists.

By the time Ivan finds me late in the day, my hand is cramped from drawing for hours.

"Draw me a dragon?" Ivan asks, sticking his arm out.

"A dragon?" The walls of my stall are covered with photos of flower designs I found online. Ornate, Indian inspired. Perfect for henna tattoos, mostly for little girls and their mothers who want to look festive for a week or so.

"A dragon with lots of fire. Try Google," says Ivan. He sits in the chair, his arm still thrust toward me like an offering. "Can you draw Smaug?"

I haven't said yes. My arm is rubbery and my fingers are stiff, but then again, it's Ivan, and he smiles a very convincing smile at me, and I haven't seen him in the last couple of days, so I tilt my head in agreement. "Okay."

I have my tablet with me, and after a short search I find a picture of Smaug good enough to paint from. I show Ivan, and he nods and settles into his chair.

I turn over his arm so the soft skin underneath shows. His arm is thick, at least twice as wide as my own, and a blue vein travels its length. His pulse shows faintly near his wrist. There are patches of salt on his skin.

"Surfing?" I ask.

"We were out on Arne's boat this morning." He rubs at the salt.

"What for?" I hand him a wet wipe from a box I have on hand.

"Wood." He rubs off the salt and holds his arm out again. The henna comes from India, via Katia's trip there last summer, in small pouches shaped like the icing bags used for decorating cakes. I choose a fresh one and poise my hand above Ivan's arm. The henna comes out smoothly, despite my stiff fingers. I can feel Ivan's eyes on me, but I don't look up. Drawing with henna takes concentration. When I'm done, I say, "Let it dry for an hour or so. It won't last long if you're in the water, surfing or whatever."

"I know," he says. He runs a finger lightly along his arm.

"Don't touch!"

"Are you done for today?" Ivan asks, dropping his hand.

There's no reason I shouldn't close up. Most other stalls are already getting pulled down, but I shake my head. "I'll stay open a little while longer."

Ivan looks around. "He's not coming, you know. I saw Bo earlier and he told me Peter had locked himself in the studio for the day."

"Yeah, well."

"Stop waiting for him, Maddie. He isn't coming."

"He might."

Ivan shakes his head. "Believe me, he's not coming. I know what I'm talking about."

"I guess," I say, though I don't want to believe him.

I unpeg all of the sarongs I've used as walls and shuffle the pictures of henna designs back into a plastic sleeve, then place everything in my market basket along with the henna tubes. The empty frame of the tent collapses onto itself by bending the poles, and the chairs fold and then slide into cases. My little piece of the exotic East disappears for the week. There are still a few people milling around the market, but I'm tired. I'm done. And Ivan's right. There's no point waiting for Peter. He's never going to come.

"You need help carrying all that," Ivan says. It's not a question.

"Bo helped me get here this morning," I say.

"Then you need help getting back."

I hand him the tent and one chair. "But keep your arm as still as you can," I say.

The market is in town, near the harbor. We could walk home through town, past Ivan's house, but that would mean I'd have to walk down the hill through the woods to my place, which would be tricky with all this stuff, so I head in the opposite direction, down a side road to the Legion Hall, then down the stairs to the beach. It's a bit longer, but there are no hills involved.

When we reach the beach, I kick off my shoes and balance them on top of the pile of stuff in my arms. We walk slowly, soaking in the sun and sand. It doesn't matter that Ivan isn't saying anything. I like having him with me.

When we reach the path to his house, I ask, "Can I come up? To be honest, I don't want to go home."

"It's that bad?"

"Peter's not too happy with me right now."

"So what? He frowns at you when he says tut-tut?"

"It's not funny, Ivan."

"I know."

My stuff is heavy. The hard plastic of the chair digs into my shoulder. "So can I come up for a bit?"

He shakes his head. "It's a disaster."

"I don't care. I haven't been in your house for years. Why is that? You always come to mine." The truth is, I think I know why I never go to his house. The place probably stinks, and I doubt if they ever do the dishes.

"Really, it's a mess," Ivan says. He stands in such a way that I'd have to push past him to get onto the path, and when I try, he shifts so he blocks it even more.

"Come on, I don't care if it's a mess."

"I do." Ivan blushes, and for the first time I see it's not that he's trying to protect me from anything; he's trying to protect himself. As if I would care that his house is a mess.

"I just want to see more than the front hall of your house. It's been ages. I can't even remember what the inside looks like. Come on."

"Another time." Ivan and I stare at each other.

"Fine," I say, and it comes out harsher than I intend it to, because I'm insulted that he thinks I would care.

"I'll clean it up soon."

"Yeah, sure. I guess I'll go home," I say as I take my stuff from him.

"You'll be fine, Maddie. Peter'll come around."

"Okay, yeah, sure." He doesn't know what it's like to live with someone who's disappointed in you. He really doesn't know.

SEVEN

Ivan

I hate lying to Maddie. And I hate being so good at it. As if I care that my house is a mess. As if she would care.

The van's not at the house when I get back from the market, which I'm glad about. Des is the last person I want to see right now. I haven't eaten all day, and I'm starving, so I pull a box of crackers out of the cupboard and scrounge around for something to put on them. There's a half-empty jar of peanut butter. It makes a good snack but only fills me up enough to remind my stomach what food's like.

The two backpacks are propped against the wall. I resist the impulse to check them until the crackers are gone, but the temptation's too strong. I lift the lid of the one closest to me and peer inside. I'm not sure what I expect to find. It's been hours since I left, after all, so Des has had lots of time to hide the stuff away from me and anyone else who might be looking. I wish I'd thought of searching earlier though.

I don't trust Pedro worth shit. Who knows what else is hidden in those baggies? It would seriously be just like Des to get involved in something sketchy without even knowing it. There's nothing in either backpack now except laundry, and I know it'll be useless trying to figure out where Des has stashed it all. He's been hiding bottles from me for years. Sometimes I find them, sometimes I don't.

My stomach growls.

There are things in the fridge: a beet, some carrots and a head of lettuce, but no matter how long I stare at them, they don't form into something I can make for dinner. Finally I give up and go to Jack's house. Jack's mother never lets me go without feeding me, and if I show up around dinnertime, she'll always invite me to stay. Besides, I'm not sure I'm strong enough to sit at the table and eat with those backpacks staring at me.

River and a couple of other guys from school stop by Jack's place after dinner, so I hang out there until everyone leaves, then head home too, opening the door as quietly as possible, checking the house over, making sure all the cigarettes in the ashtray are properly out before slipping into my room without turning on any of the lights. It's been a long day. I don't need any more shit from Des.

*   *   *

For the next week, Des and I circle each other. I know he's around, because every day when I come back from writing my finals, the pile of dishes in the sink grows, as does the pile of bottles in the bin. By the third day the backpacks are gone. I don't know whether I'm trying to run into him or trying to avoid him. When school is finally over, I spend my days working on Bo's shelving and helping him dismantle the remains of the burned shed. Bo says he'll hire me to build a new one, which would be great. We need every penny I can make. I keep expecting Des to show up with some money, but he never does. Not for the first time, I'm grateful that Des inherited the house from my grandmother and we only have to pay the taxes on it every year.

On Saturday morning I hear Des rustling in the bathroom, so I get up and there he is, standing in front of the mirror, shaving. His eyes look clear in the reflection, though I heard him coming in late last night, so I say, "What are you doing?"

He scrapes the razor over his cheek, pulling a streak of shaving cream with it. "Good morning to you too," he says.

"I want some of the money."

He leans in to peer at his face. Runs his hand over his cheek to make sure he got all the stubble. He doesn't answer.

"Groceries, Des. I need money for food. And toilet paper would be good. And soap."

He nods but doesn't say anything as he shaves the other cheek.

I straighten, trying to take up as much of the doorway as possible. "Des, give me some money."

He runs water over the razor until the foam and hair swill around in the sink. "I spent it," he says.

"What? What the hell did you spend it on? Not food, that's for sure."

"I had debts. And don't worry, I'll get groceries. And toilet paper. And soap. In case you haven't noticed, I'm going to work today." He looks at me through the mirror.

It's true. He has on a clean shirt and pants with no holes or anything. Even his socks match.

"Seriously?"

"Yes, seriously."

"So you were telling the truth when you said you were looking for a job? That's what you've been doing all week?"

"Of course I was. When have I ever lied to you?"

"Yeah right."

"Look, I'm meeting some guys today about a job. It's going to be fine." He rubs a towel across his face and runs his fingers through his hair. He smooths down his shirt and hangs the towel back on the rack. "Now move. I'm going to be late."

I jump out of the doorway to let him pass.

* * *

I spend the morning working. It's possible Des *has* gotten a job. Maybe he *is* going to buy groceries. But probably he isn't. Time will tell. Right now, I like spending time with my saw and a fresh plank of cedar. I love the way the cedar smell hits the air when I shave off a sliver of wood. The smoothness of it when it's sanded; even the way the sawdust gets caught in the sunbeams and floats around. That thought makes me chuckle: I sound like Maddie.

I'm halfway through measuring when Des comes home. He sits on the step and slurps a cup of coffee.

"Do you have to sit there and watch me?" I ask. I was enjoying being alone. Having him here puts an edge on things.

"What should I do then?" he says.

I'm about to say *go away*, but then I think better of it and say, "You could help."

"But you're doing such a good job," he says.

"Still."

He puts his cup down and stretches. "All right, hand me the tape measure."

We've done this for years, ever since I was old enough to hold a hammer and nails, and there's a rhythm between us that feels easy. When we work together, Des and I get along.

Des whistles as he works. I tell him about a white whale in Russia that Bo told me about.

"No shit," he says. "Arne told me about a black bear that's got so used to the dump, the other day it ambled in, found a sofa someone dropped off and sat himself right down on it. Check it out," he says, showing me a picture on his phone.

It doesn't take long before the shelf we're working on is finished.

"Thanks for your help," I say as I wrap the cords and make sure all the bits are in the box. He sweeps up the sawdust.

"So what's the job?" I ask.

"What job?"

"The one you went to this morning."

"Oh yeah."

I snap the box of bits shut. "What do you mean, *oh yeah*? That's not an answer."

He laughs. "Don't be so worried. I'm doing transport and distribution."

"Of what?" I don't like the sound of this at all, and my voice comes out rough.

"Calm down. Of goods. Mostly for grocery and hardware stores."

That sounds okay. I stop and look at him to make sure he's not lying. He doesn't look away when I catch his eye.

"So we are going to get some groceries?"

"I said we would, didn't I?"

"Yeah." He's said many things. "There are other bills too—we still owe for the repairs on the septic system," I say.

"No problem," he says. "And after a while I'll have paid off all my debts and I'll get back to working with wood. We'll work together. Partners."

"Sure," I say, because though I don't want to be enough of a sucker to believe him, there's something in me that already does.

"Relax, Ivan. I'll get paid at the end of the week, and I swear that you can personally walk me to the grocery store. I will buy soap, toilet paper, bread, milk, juice, those nasty pepperoni sticks you like, some apples…"

"Okay, okay. I get it. We'll get groceries."

"We will," he says. "I promise we will."

Well, shit. I guess I'm going to have to believe him.

EIGHT

Maddie

"Peter wants us to talk," Bo says when I pop into the living room on Sunday morning to say I'm leaving. He's settled into writing for the day; already there are books open all over his desk.

"Do we have to?"

"He's in the shower, so if you leave now, you might be able to miss him. I'll cover for you."

I run into the room and engulf Bo in a huge hug. "Thank you," I say into his hair.

I jog up to the road and text Ivan to see what he's up to. He's been helping Bo out back with the shed, but we haven't had any time to hang out together, which is unusual. We agree to meet on the beach.

"You look happy," I say when we both reach the root that marks the midway point between our houses.

"Finally finished those shelves Bo ordered."

"He'll be glad."

"Yeah, I'm pretty happy with them. What are you up to?" he says.

"Delivering invitations to the Lazy Days party. I like to get them out early so no one makes plans."

He laughs. "Maddie, no one in Bear Harbour or anywhere in a hundred-mile radius is going to make plans for that weekend. Your parties are famous."

I like this happy Ivan. The smile that reaches his eyes.

He takes an invitation from the box I'm carrying and looks at the scene I've painted on it. A fire on the beach, people sitting on logs, Ivan and me laughing behind them. When he looks up, his smile covers even more of his face.

"You painted us."

"You like it?"

Ivan holds the card up and examines it like it's a famous painting. "I do," he says, and then he asks, "So this is still going ahead, even with Peter and everything?"

"Yes." We've held a Lazy Days party in the summer every year since I was eight. No way we're going to cancel just because we're all stressing out.

"Need some help delivering? Des is doing something with Arne today. They went off in Arne's boat, so I have the van. It's at the dock in town, I just have to pick it up," Ivan says.

"That's awesome. I was going to walk."

Ivan looks at me like I'm crazy, and it's true. It would take days to deliver all these cards on foot.

* * *

Ivan and I spend the morning delivering invitations to everyone in town and even a few people living in the coves and bays nearby. It's fun spending the morning together. Des's van has a pretty good music system, even though it's old, so we take turns plugging in our phones and choosing what to listen to. Ivan has some music from way back when we were kids, which is pretty funny, and people walking by must think we're weirdos singing along to Fred Penner at the top of our lungs.

When all the invitations are delivered, Ivan says, "Let's go to Scottie's. I'll buy you a drink."

"No way. You just spent ages driving me around. I'll buy you a drink."

He puts the van in Park and reaches past me into the glove compartment. He pulls a twenty out of a tin.

"I know where Des keeps a bit of cash." Ivan chuckles and winks at me, which makes me laugh.

"Nice."

We're still laughing when we go into Scottie's and walk to the back where the drinks are.

"Coke or chocolate milk?" Ivan says.

"Orange juice, please."

He reaches into the fridge and pulls out a bottle of juice and a carton of chocolate milk. "Snacks?" he asks.

"You choose."

We wander through the aisles. He points to a bag of salt-and-pepper chips and I nod, and then we go to the candy section.

"Hey, Willow," Ivan says to a small girl. She runs down the aisle and throws herself at him, and he grunts when he catches her in his arms. "Wow, you're getting big," he says.

"I am. I weigh thirty-eight pounds, and I bet I'm going to be forty pounds when I turn six."

"I bet you are."

She holds up a fistful of gummy bears and says, "Grandpa said I could have candy."

"Nice grandpa," says Ivan.

"Is she your girlfriend?" Willow says, pointing at me.

"Nah," Ivan says, and he gives me a funny look. It's starting to feel super awkward, but then Pedro comes around the counter, looking for Willow.

"Hey, Ivan," he says.

"What are you doing in town, Pedro?"

"Came to meet Des for some business. Didn't he tell you?"

Ivan shakes his head. The way his eyebrows bunch together and his mouth goes thin tells me everything I need to know about how Ivan feels about Pedro.

"What kind of business?" Ivan's voice is so heavy it drops onto the ground.

"Don't worry, Ivan, it's fine. Des is going to be working with the Salmon Festival. He asked me to help. That's all." He tries to pat Ivan on the shoulder, but Ivan flinches away.

"Who asked him to help with the Salmon Festival?" says Ivan.

Pedro shakes his head and shrugs. "No idea. Someone."

Willow shoves her way between Ivan and Pedro and thrusts her fist into Pedro's face. "Grandpa, can I have these ones?"

"Sure. One fistful, I said."

Willow bounces up and down. "Look what I get to have!" she says.

Ivan gives her a high five before she and Pedro go to pay for the candy, but as soon as she leaves, his face goes flat, like the person inside it walked away.

"What?" I ask.

He shakes his head and walks back into his face. This is the Ivan I usually see, but… "Come on, Ivan, what's up? You don't like that guy."

"It's nothing. You want candy, or is this enough?"

The smile doesn't reach his eyes.

"Ivan."

"It's nothing," he says. "Let's get gummy bears. I love gummy bears."

I let him scoop out gummy bears and licorice. He plays with the gummy bears and pulls on the licorice and gulps at his chocolate milk, but I don't play along, because I feel like I've been punched between the eyes.

That flat face, so quickly controlled.

Gummy bears, so sweet they put my teeth on edge.

NINE

Ivan

Just once I'd like to believe Des and have that be the right thing to do. Just once. Here he is, back from his outing with Arne, sitting on the sofa and smiling at me over his laptop like I'm a kid who knows nothing.

"Des," I shout at him from the doorway.

"What're you shouting about?"

"Pedro. I thought you were done with him."

He slurps something.

"I saw Pedro in town. He told me some bullshit about you being hired to do something for the Salmon Festival."

Des slams his computer shut and stands up.

"Why can't you ever believe in me?" he asks. He points his finger at my face and says, "Bo asked me to build a stage for him, for out front of the library. For your infor-fucking-mation."

I take a step back. "And Pedro? Why's he here?"

"To help me." He sinks back down into the sofa and pulls the computer onto his lap, knocking over a beer bottle in the process.

He's drunk. Awesome.

"Why didn't you ask me?" I say. I'm still standing in the doorway. Seems like a good place to stay.

He peers over the top of his screen. "What?"

I take a deep breath and say again, "Why didn't you ask me to help you?"

He stares for a minute, his eyes droopy, then looks back at the screen. He has no answer, just as I thought.

"You want to know why I don't believe in you. Well, maybe it's because you don't ever believe in me." I grab my sweater and storm back out the door.

I stomp down to the beach, heading nowhere in particular, just away from Des. It feels like shit to be duped all the time. What a fucking idiot I am.

I should leave. Really, really, I should pack up and walk away.

It's only because of the way Des cries in his sleep that I don't. And a memory or two from long ago. Oh, and the small fact that he'd probably burn down the house with himself inside if he was left alone. I shouldn't let these things keep me here, but like I said, I'm an idiot.

I don't see Maddie until her red skirt comes into view and she's pacing along with me. "Stop," she says.

I don't. I can't face Maddie right now.

"Stop." She pulls on my shoulder and spins me around.

"What?"

"What are you upset about?"

"Mind your own business, Maddie." I turn away from her and continue along the beach. After ten steps I stop and spin around to face her. "Did Bo ask Des to make a stage for the Salmon Festival?" I ask.

"I don't know."

I turn away again and keep walking, but this time she calls after me, "Ivan, do you have to be so angry? Can't you let it go?"

"What do you think I'm doing?" I shout back at her. I keep going down the beach, and she doesn't follow me.

When I've walked the beach back and forth three times, I slow down and head over to Maddie's house. She's sitting on the deck with two cups steaming next to her.

"Yes, he did," she says when I step onto the deck.

"He did?"

"Yep. I asked."

She hands me a mug and wraps her hands around her own. I sit on the log that makes a railing and take a sip. Sweet hot chocolate fills my mouth. Maddie's smiling at me because she thinks she's given me the right answer. I smile back because I don't feel like explaining. We sit together and drink hot chocolate and watch the waves. I like that about Maddie, how we can sit together and not say anything.

When I'm done my drink, I put the mug down and say, "What are you doing now?"

"River's coming by a bit later to borrow a board. You know he broke the fin on his when he went to Tofino last week."

"Surfing. Perfect," I say.

Maddie stands and says, "Let's go get your stuff."

I tip my mug up so the chocolate sludge at the bottom slides into my mouth. I don't want to go home. "How about I just use something here, an old suit of Bo's or something?"

"Sure. We've got lots of old suits. Even one that used to be Peter's. Something here'll fit. And there's lots of boards."

Maddie goes inside and comes back out a couple of minutes later in her bathing suit. She leads me around the house to one of the sheds at the back. The burned one is gone now, and we've piled up wood for building a new one, but the stink of fire stirs as we walk past. She pulls open the door to the shed they keep their gear in, and the fug of old wet suits fills the air, replacing the smoke.

"There must be something in here," she says.

The room is filled with wet suits, life jackets, paddles, spray skirts, all hanging on pegs on the walls. She pulls a suit off a peg and tosses it to me. "Try this."

There's no privacy from her in here. I've always been careful to wear long shorts when I'm surfing, longer than the boxers I'm wearing right now. Goose bumps rise on my arms as I pull off my clothes. I try to get my wet suit over my legs as quickly as possible, while she's got her head in a pile of her own gear, but I'm not fast enough. She glances over at me while I'm still half naked. Her intake of breath is audible. She steps forward and runs her hand along an old scar on my thigh. The flesh tingles. She's about to ask. I can see the question in her eyes, but then River's face appears in the doorway.

"Maddie, you coming out? I need a board. Can I use that old one I had the other day?" he says.

Maddie tosses her hair and lets her hand drop, then grabs her suit from the peg and shoves her legs into it.

"Hey, Ivan. You guys ready?" River asks.

I turn around and pull my suit up over my chest. Maddie points to a board on the wall, and I take it down and follow her and River out of the shed and onto the path to the beach.

She'll ask her question later, I know it. I'm going to have to think about how I'll answer.

TEN

Maddie

Surfing is fun. We lie on our boards and wait for the waves. The fog comes in, turning everything soft and slow, and silence flows easy between us. A lone seal joins us in the waves, and we take turns riding them with him. Then Jack and Noah arrive, and it starts to feel crowded, especially because Jack insists on giving Noah surfing tips, which he does by shouting a running commentary with every wave Noah catches. It's nice of Jack to do this, but it spoils the mood.

"I'm heading home," I say to Ivan when I'm tired of listening to Jack. He nods and waves and catches a sweet ride.

At home, once I'm dry and changed, I head to my bedroom and pull out my paints. It's late afternoon, and the light bounces off the roof of Peter's studio and catches the lichen hanging off the trees. A raven rests on a branch, looking out toward the sea until Peter bangs the studio door, and then it caws angrily.

The painted raven takes shape in front of me, angry, sharp beak turned to me like a knife, ready to strike, but wings like an angel's, bright and fierce. The light fades, but I keep painting, trying to capture its movement, keep the tension between light and dark, sharp and soft, angel and wild beast. My hand flows, inspired by the fog-suffused light and my afternoon surfing and something else I can't put my finger on. It's my best work yet.

Peter wanders into the room when I'm almost done. He has the scent of resin around him, and that air of coming back from far away that he gets when he's been working on a new violin. He sits on my bed and watches me. "It's good to see you working on real paintings, Maddie," he says.

I don't answer, but I do stand back so he can look at what I've done. He stares at it, his eyes wandering over each section of the painting. "It's good," he says, but there's no conviction in his voice.

"But?"

"But nothing. It's good."

"You can say it," I say.

"Here," he says, pointing to the tail. "There's something missing."

"Yeah, I know. I'm working on it."

Peter nods. "It's good though. This is what you should be spending your time on."

"I am spending time on it," I say. I'd like to keep working on the tail, but it's hard to concentrate with him here.

"I mean real time, instead of those whatever-you-call-them you're wasting your time with at the market."

"The henna tattoos, do you mean?" My voice has gone chilly.

"This is what you should be spending your time on, Maddie," he repeats.

"I made almost three hundred dollars on Saturday," I say.

Peter snorts. "Three hundred dollars? You think that's enough?"

"It's a start."

"But that's not the point, is it? Are you going to spend the rest of your life painting henna tattoos when you could be doing this kind of thing instead?" Peter waves his arm at my painting.

"Don't be such a snob, Peter. What's wrong with tattoos?"

Peter shakes his head and says, "My God, you're infuriating, Maddie. You have so much talent. I don't know why you don't want to take it somewhere."

"I do, just not the way you want me to. Can't you trust me?"

"It's not about trust. It's about experience, knowledge, being open to learning and new ideas."

"Oh, for God's sake, Peter, leave me alone. I don't want to go to university right now. Why can't you understand that?"

"You're too young to truly know what you want, Maddie. When I was your age, I was totally lost. I wish I'd had someone help me out. That's all we're trying to do."

"Well, that was you," I say. "This is me, and I know what I want." This conversation feels so repetitive. How often are we going to have to have it?

Peter throws his arms up dramatically and leaves the room. I try to go back to my painting, but I can't concentrate anymore. He's ruined it for me.

I take the painting into the living room to see if the light's better there. There's only one surfer still at the far end of the bay, too far away for me to see him clearly, but it's got to be Ivan. He'll stay there for hours, long past when everyone else goes home. When I see him, I realize what the other element was that kept me painting, the thing sitting in my mind that I couldn't put my finger on. The scar. The one I saw this afternoon. It's a bad one, not something a person could easily hide, and it must be from something that happened several years ago, judging by how faded it is. No one knew about it, and I don't understand why not. How could someone hide an injury like that? Why would they?

And it makes me wonder what other things Ivan's hiding. That flat, controlled face I saw this morning. It makes me shiver to think about it, or, rather, to think about why he needs it. What kind of life makes you good at shutting down? What's going on that I don't know about? What kind of injury made that scar?

"Peter tells me I have to look at your painting," says Bo, interrupting my musing. He stands in front of the painting with his hand on his chin. "He's right. This is one of your best," he says.

"That's what he said?"

"I like the juxtaposition of the fierceness of the beak and the grace of the wings," he says.

Which is what I was aiming for. I leave the window seat and stand beside him. We both ponder the painting.

"I need to work on this area." I touch the tail of the bird and the sky behind.

Bo nods. "But the rest of it—spectacular. What are you going to do with it?"

"I need to finish it before I decide anything like that."

"Peter would be very happy if you finished it and, you know, showed it somewhere."

"Yeah." My voice sounds bitter, even to my ears.

"Whoa. Don't bite my head off. Don't show it if you don't want to." Bo puts his arm around me. "You know you don't have to. You don't have to go to university either, not if you don't want to."

I lean into him. Bo, my rock. Somehow I can never stay mad at him, even for a minute. I can never hide things from him either. "Bo, did you ever hear Des talk about Ivan injuring himself?"

He laughs. "Ivan's always injuring himself."

"No, I mean *really* injuring himself. A broken leg or something like that."

"Not that I can remember. Why? Has he shown up with a broken leg?"

"No. Just something he said. It's nothing."

"Speaking of Ivan, you know, Maddie, that tattoo of Smaug you made for him. It was very creative. I think you might have a future as a tattoo artist." Bo says this with a straight face, but then we both laugh at the idea.

"Can you imagine Peter's reaction if I told him I was going to be a tattoo artist?"

"It's just because he sees how much talent you have. You know that, right? He just wants what's best for you."

"What *he* thinks is best for me. I don't know what's best for me yet."

"I know. University is a good first step though. You can't help but learn a lot."

"I know. I'll think about it. But maybe you guys can just trust me, you know?"

"I'll think about it." Bo laughs and kisses the top of my head. "Leave this painting here while you work on it. I like how it looks in the room," he says. He sits at his work table and picks up a book, and with that action he disappears. I've always envied Bo's ability to engage completely and immediately with his work.

I try to do the same, but the passion for the painting is gone, at least for now.

That scar. My mind keeps coming back to the scar.

ELEVEN

Ivan

They're all on the deck when I go down to Maddie's house to return the board and suit from yesterday and pick up the clothes I left in the shed. Maddie's done this awesome painting of a raven—I can see it through the window.

"Hey, I'm here for my clothes," I say.

"They're still in the shed," Maddie says, so I lean the board up against the rack next to the house and head back to the shed to get them.

Maddie follows. I know what's coming. "That scar." She creases her brow in a way that makes her look exactly like Peter. "What happened?"

"It was years ago."

She opens the door to the shed. "You were a kid? How come none of us knew?"

"It was just after my mom left. It was an accident."

"But that doesn't explain how come none of us knew."

"It's just…it was an accident. I fell over and landed in a pile of firewood. One of the pieces speared my leg." What I don't say: Des was drunk, and even though it was an accident, we thought if people knew they might take me away from him. If they thought he couldn't take care of me.

"So you hid it? Didn't Des take you to the clinic?"

"Des is good at that kind of thing. He cleaned it up and bandaged it and everything. He even put in a couple of stitches. It looks a lot worse than it was."

My clothes are still in the pile I left them in, and I just want to take them and go, but Maddie's still looking at me with that crease between her eyes. It's a Maddie look, one I know well. Usually I love to see it, because it means she's sorting out a problem in her mind. It reminds me how smart this girl is. But today I turn away from it, because I don't want her to dwell on what I've just said, and I curse myself. I've raised a question in Maddie's mind about me and Des that I didn't want to raise. Stupid me for letting her see that scar. I should have known. I should have fucking known.

* * *

When I get back to my place, I hear Des before I see him as I walk out of the path from the beach and into our yard. He's got the saw out and is cutting into a two-by-four. He's whistling.

"Hold on to this, will you?" he asks as I come into view.

"How come you're in such a good mood?"

"I like working," he says. He's about to screw two pieces together into a T, so he points to where he wants me to brace the wood. He leans over the drill, using his weight to help the screws drive in faster.

"What're you building?" I ask.

"Frame for the stage."

"You're building it here? Doesn't it need to be made in place?"

"The space isn't cleared yet, so we'll build the frame here, then take it in pieces over there when they're ready for us," he says.

"And where's Pedro? How come he isn't helping you?"

"He's doing other stuff."

"What other stuff?"

Des drives in the last screw and straightens up. He puts the drill down and stretches before he says, "He's meeting some folks about the space. There's debris that needs to be cleared away."

"Isn't it a bit early?" I ask.

"This is when they wanted to meet him," Des says.

He keeps working, and I sit down on a stool to watch. He starts whistling again, and it occurs to me that maybe he's telling the truth. Maybe he is trying to get his act together, and he is doing this thing for Bo, and maybe Pedro really is off figuring out how to clear up the trash, and just maybe things are going to be better around here.

TWELVE

Maddie

It's been a couple of weeks since I painted the raven Bo likes so much. Peter and I have been tiptoeing around each other ever since. Bo says I need to give Peter time to adjust to the idea of me making my own way in the world. I understand what he's saying, but I wish Peter would get over it. I've decided to save money for a flight to Paris. I'm going to live in a hostel and spend my days in the galleries. That's how you study art.

It's a sunny morning, though, and I love this time of year, when the village swells into a town and everything's growing so fast you can almost see it creeping in through windows and around corners. This morning I have to push aside a branch of salal to close my window. Bo will be furious; he hates when the salal grows over the pathways, and he fights it every year, but it makes me laugh. Even now, three weeks after the shed burned down, there's the stink of fire everywhere, and the scent of fresh green growth makes me sit up and smile.

"Fish and chips?" asks Bo when I go into the living room. "Jane's opens today. First fishing tours came in. Jane's will be hopping."

I hold up my coffee cup and yawn. "It's only 8:30, a bit early for fish and chips."

"I meant for lunch. We could all go." Bo, ever the peacemaker.

"Peter's coming?"

"It'll be nice, the three of us together."

"Sure," I say, because I do love Jane's.

I told Alice, Noah's mom, that I'd help her in her garden first thing, and I told Katia and another school friend, Bea, that I'd meet them for coffee, so I arrange to meet Bo and Peter on the dock at noon and head out.

The walk to Noah's house is full of the scents of summer, and I whistle as I walk. My plan is to pay for the fish and chips at Jane's today, to show Peter and Bo that I'm serious about making some money.

There are cars parked along the road and in the driveway at Noah's. I wasn't counting on that. I was looking forward to a bit of quiet time in Alice's garden, helping her plant her veggies.

"We've got a painting party going on," says Alice when I find her shoveling a pile of topsoil onto her garden bed.

"Looks like a lot of people."

"It's amazing. People here are so helpful—it's been just wonderful. Everyone's come out." Her face is full of smiles.

"Where did you move from again?"

"Toronto. But we'd been there for years and hardly knew our neighbors at all, and we've only been here a few months and already we know everyone, and so many people turned out to paint the shed." She seems so happy.

"Remind me not to move to Toronto," I say with a laugh.

We walk around to the back of the house to get some tools for me. Noah's thirteen-year-old sister, Laurie, and a couple of other girls are doing cartwheels and handstands on the lawn.

"Hey, Maddie," they call.

"What's up?"

"We're practicing," says Laurie.

"We're going to busk on the dock this summer," says Kyra, Jack's little sister.

"Are you?"

Alice laughs and says in a low voice, "If they can find something they're talented at."

There are a lot of people here. Arne and Jack are standing at the bottom of the shed looking up, and Noah's standing on the roof looking down at them.

"That doesn't look like painting," I say, pointing to Noah.

"Uh, no. The shed's leaking, and it seemed pointless to paint until the roof was fixed, so they're starting with the roof."

"Is it safe?"

"Arne insists it is, and it's not that high."

"I guess." I hate seeing people standing on roofs. Looking up at them gives me vertigo.

Alice and I settle into raking the new topsoil and planting lettuce and spinach and kale. It's a bit late for them, but they should be okay as long as they're kept moist. Her soil is good, and it doesn't take long to get the seedlings planted.

"Thanks, Maddie," Alice says when we're done. "Would you like something to drink?"

"Please," I say.

When she goes into the house, I wander across the yard to check out the shed. Noah's off the roof, and he and Jack and Arne have joined Des and Ivan inside.

Des is painting the wall with a roller. Ivan's standing halfway up a ladder, brushing into the corner.

I stand in the shadow of the doorway and watch Ivan finish. He climbs down the ladder. As he steps off it, it wobbles and he stumbles, but Des reaches out and steadies him. It's a gesture any dad would make, but when Des touches him, Ivan flinches like an ember has landed on his skin.

"Clumsy," says Des.

Jack laughs and says to Noah, "Ivan is the clumsiest person I've ever met."

But...

He surfs like a seal.

He has a scar on his leg that no one knows about.

Ivan and Des share a glance, and for a second, half a second, a fraction of a second, I see it. The flat face with no one behind it. Then he shrugs and says, "Sometimes."

But...what am I seeing? Is this a sign of how things are between Des and Ivan? Where did that scar really come from?

It's like looking at Des and Ivan for the first time, and it's a slap in my face. A hard one. On the one hand, there are all those times Des has helped us out. So many times over the years. But then there are also all the times Ivan comes to our house hungry. How we're never sure what job Des is currently on. How Ivan never lets me or anyone else into his house. All the little clues I never put together, never thought much of, because that's just the way it is. Des is a fuckup. We all know that. He and Ivan bumble along. We all know that. But now I wonder if there's something else there, and it makes me sick to my stomach to think about it.

But then Des puts his hand on Ivan's shoulder and pulls him into a sideways hug. "It comes from your mother's side," he says, and everyone laughs, including Ivan.

So maybe I'm mistaken.

Maybe I am.

THIRTEEN

Ivan

Des and I finish helping Noah and his family with their shed and walk down to the dock for some lunch at Jane's. People are milling around, waiting for their orders to be ready. There's a lineup of people like us who've come in from all around for their first fish and chips of the season. It's a ritual. It's how we know summer is really here.

"Two pieces of halibut and some fries, please," I say when I get to the counter. "And a Coke." I pull my wallet out of my pocket out of habit, but Des elbows me in the ribs. "Hey, I'm buying."

I take a plastic cup and go to the side of the stall to pour myself a glass of Coke. A waist-high girl of four or five lifts her cup up but can't quite reach the lever to pull it herself.

"Can I help you?" I ask.

She nods and hands me her cup.

"What do you want?"

"7-Up," she says.

I fill her cup—not too full, so she won't spill it—and hand it back to her. She smiles at me and walks over to her family, carrying the cup in both hands.

While we wait for our fish to be ready, Des and I sit on the dock. Among the crowd are Bo, Peter, Maddie, Bea and Katia. Bo sees us and waves us over.

"I see you've been painting." Bo points to the streak of white paint along my arm.

"We were helping out Noah and his family with their shed," I say.

When our orders are called, Des and Bo go get the food and come back carrying our baskets. Noah and Laurie are with them, and the little girl I got a drink for follows them, carrying a plastic bag in her hand. She opens the bag and takes out a piece of fish, which she holds over the water. A snout and whiskers appear out of nowhere and snatch it from her.

"Holy shit, what was that?" asks Noah.

"That was Luseal," Maddie says.

Laurie peers over the dock, "Look," she says, and we all lean over the edge in time to see a flash of silver streak by.

"Luseal is a harbor seal. She's lived here for years," I say.

The girl takes another piece of fish out of the bag and holds it in the air again. Noah and Laurie lean over with her, waiting for the flash of whiskers and teeth.

"Do you want to try?" the little girl asks Laurie after the seal has taken the fish, but Laurie says, "No, it's okay. I'll watch you."

When the little girl holds up the fish this time, there is no movement in the water, so she leans farther out, calling, "Luseal, come get the fish."

There are a lot of people on the dock now, and I can see Pedro walking toward us.

Des hands me his empty basket and says, "I'll see you later, Ivan," then shoves his way through a bunch of tourists toward Pedro. I'm just wondering about that when a boat comes in too fast, and its wake sends a spray of water over the clump of people on the dock. They surge away from the water, and someone steps back into the little girl. She lurches, her arms flailing, then splashes into the water.

"Holy shit," says Noah. He slams to the dock and reaches out for her, but I already know that's not going to work. The current's not strong here in the harbor, but the tide's flooding, so it'll pull her toward the shore, under the dock. She's so little. Does she know how to swim? There's a man shouting at us, probably her dad, but there are so many people in the way, he's having a hard time making it through the crowd.

The little girl's still flailing; I kick off my shoes and jump in after her. The shock of the cold water sends pins and needles to my brain, but I force myself to open my eyes. I can see for a few feet in front of me, but behind me it's dark in the shadow of the dock. I swivel, looking for the girl, and see her feet flapping around just as they disappear into the darkness ten feet away from me. My fingers are going numb, but I swim toward her. When I reach where I think she is, I rise up, take a deep breath and dive under.

It's hard to see anything under the dock, so I swim with my arms sweeping ahead of me until I bump into something that feels like clothing and grasp it with my fingers. As I pull her toward me, she claws at me, so I have to wrap my arms around hers. Her hair tangles in front of my eyes, and she struggles to get free of my grasp. My lungs are swollen and I'm fighting to keep my mouth from opening, but my brain kicks in and tells my legs to push off the pylon and head toward the light.

As soon as we're out from under the dock, we rise and both of us gasp for air. The little girl screams and grabs me around the neck, threatening to send me under again, and I have to pull at her arms to keep her from choking me. There's a flash of movement at the other end of the dock as Luseal heads toward us. The girl is screaming in my ear and tearing at my hair, and it's all I can do to tread water fast enough to keep from sinking.

"Get her out," I yell at the arms stretched out to us, and someone grabs a handful of her shirt and an arm and pulls her up. Other hands take me by the shoulders and pull until I'm sitting on the edge of the dock. I raise my legs out of the water just as Luseal streaks past. The thought of her teeth makes me shiver. Luseal may be cute when you're standing on the dock, but she's way too fond of snapping her teeth at whatever comes her way for my liking.

There's a blanket across my shoulders, and someone's rubbing my arms. I can't think of anything but breathing and blinking away the stinging in my eyes. My fingers and toes are numb. Sometimes, late in the summer, it's okay to swim here a bit, but it hasn't been that warm and sunny so far, and the water still feels like liquid ice cubes.

"You saved her life," Noah says. He hands me a cup of hot chocolate, which I hold in both hands for the warmth.

Des sits down on my other side. "You okay, buddy?" he asks. He puts his arm around me and pulls me into a hug. His body is warm and big.

"Yeah, just cold."

"You're a hero," says Noah, to make me laugh.

"How is she?" I ask.

"She's fine," says Noah. "Her dad took her up to their car to get some warm clothes on."

"Her family should have come to see how Ivan is," says Maddie, who's joined us. She hands me another cup of hot chocolate, replacing the old one though I haven't drunk any of it.

"Drink this one," she says.

My fingers are so numb I can hardly move them, so I just hold on to the cup until she lifts it to my mouth, and then I take a sip. The heat seeps through me.

"Let's get you home, buddy," Des says.

I take a few more sips of the hot chocolate. My fingers and toes are burning, but the rest of me is shivering, and it's hard to control my legs enough to stand. I have to stomp my feet a few times before I can make my legs move enough to walk. My teeth are chattering, and my whole body shakes with cold. Maddie takes my hand and pulls me along the dock, followed by Des and Bo and Peter and Noah and Laurie.

People move out of the way as we walk past. They're talking about me; I can tell by the way they stare. They probably think I fell in. Whatever. Let them think what they want.

As we reach the parking lot a woman runs up to me.

"Thank you, thank you," she says. She takes my hand and presses it in both of hers. She's crying. "You saved her life." She wipes her eyes, but it doesn't seem to make any difference, as the tears keep pouring down her face.

I smile at her and let her hold my hand. "Someone else would have gone after her if I didn't."

"I think he needs to get home," Des says.

"Oh, yes, of course," the woman says. "Thank you, I can't thank you enough. Before you go, tell me your name."

"It's Ivan," says Des. He puts his arm on my shoulder and steers me toward the road.

I smile at the woman again.

*   *   *

"In you go," Des says when we reach the house. He opens the door for me, and I make a beeline for the shower, standing under the hot water until it runs out. My fingers have thawed, but I'm still cold inside.

"Made you a cup of coffee," Des says when I eventually join him outside.

We sit together on our bar stools while I sip the coffee.

"Maybe we'll rent a movie this evening, eh?" Des says.

"And I'll make you some mac and cheese, your favorite."

"Sounds great." It shouldn't be such a big deal, but the whole experience shook me, if I'm being honest, and a quiet evening sounds about right to me. When I'm done my coffee, I head inside to find a warmer sweater. On my way back down the stairs I hear voices, and when I walk outside, Pedro is sitting on my stool.

"We're headed over to Sayward Harbour for the evening," he says.

I look at Des, but he won't meet my eye. He's got his wallet in one hand and car key in the other.

"I thought we were watching a movie and you were making dinner," I say.

"Another time, eh?"

"Is there food? Something I can make dinner with?"

"Must be. I'm sure there is. You didn't want to spend the evening with me anyway, did you?"

"Actually, I did. At least, I wanted you to make me dinner."

Pedro laughs. "Kids, eh? Always wanting something."

Des laughs with him and grabs his coat from the peg on the wall. "Make sure to stay warm, Ivan. And don't expect me back tonight," he says as he walks through the door.

89

FOURTEEN

Maddie

Ivan's already pretty drunk when I see him later at Jack's house. It's Jack's parents' twentieth wedding anniversary, and practically the whole town has been invited. There's champagne and lox and strawberries inside, and a keg out back. Someone's made a huge cake with two plastic people in wedding gear standing on top, and it sits in the middle of the dining-room table.

Kyra and Laurie and their friends are in the living room, dancing to some hippie New Age music with lots of drums and flutes.

"Hi, Maddie," Kyra calls out as I weave through the swaying crowd.

I talk to her for a bit, until Ivan comes up behind me and says, "Hey, Maddie, there you are. Come outside with me," and I follow him to the back patio. Jack, River and Noah are already in the hot tub, along with some other kids from the high school, people I don't really know. But I am pretty sure they'll be slobbery beer drinkers I don't want to spend time with.

"Hey, we were waiting for you guys," shouts Jack when we get there.

"What for?" I ask.

Noah holds up a bottle of tequila. "We haven't even opened it yet. We were waiting for the hero," he says.

Ivan laughs and walks around to the back of the hot tub, where he strips to his board shorts, which, I notice for the first time ever, are long and cover his scar. He slides into the tub. Too fast. Too far away. Too interested in tequila. He and Noah unscrew the cap and swig from the bottle. I stand at the side of the hot tub and let the steam wash over me.

"Come on in, Maddie," Jack says. He shoves the guy next to him to make room for me, but I can see the bottle of tequila doing the rounds, and Ivan's already slouched in an I'm-not-moving-from-here position on the other side of the tub. He doesn't meet my eye when I look at him, so I shake my head and go back into the house.

I chill with the girls for a while, swaying and dancing to their music, but they're kids and they giggle a lot, so after a while I go to the dining room to get some food. Bea and Katia are there, so I stay and talk to them. Bea's heading off to McGill in a few weeks, and Katia's going to Victoria for nursing school. I haven't told them, or anyone else, that I got into Emily Carr but am not going. I'm afraid they'd also look at me like I'm insane.

When I finish a plate of bagels and lox and strawberries and have had a couple of glasses of champagne, I excuse myself and head back outside to tell Ivan I'm leaving with Bea and Katia. The boys are still in the hot tub, staring at the stars. I make my way around the hot tub until I'm standing next to Ivan.

"I'm going," I say. There are so many things I'm not saying with those words. Many things.

"Aw, come on, why? The evening's just getting going."

"You're drunk."

He looks at me and frowns. "No I'm not."

"You are."

"Yeah, I am. Come get drunk with me." He pats the seat next to him, but his head lolls unappealingly on the side of the hot tub, and I back away.

"Whatever, Ivan. I'll see you later."

Enough with the drunk boys. Bea and Katia and I head to Bea's house, on the other side of the harbor. We've taken a bottle of champagne with us for the walk.

"Ivan's really hot, Maddie. You should totally go for him," Katia says. She's been saying this since about the eighth grade, so I ignore her.

"He is," Bea says.

"You know we're, like, best friends," I say to them. "I've known him since forever."

"So what? All the better." Katia shoves my shoulder playfully, and I stumble into the road.

"Come on, you guys. He's Ivan. I mean, we used to take baths together, and Bo taught us both how to tie our shoes. He's like my brother or something."

"And he's super hot. And you know everything about him. You know him better than anyone. What could be more perfect?" Katia says.

Tears fill my eyes. Even a week ago I might have agreed with her, that Ivan and I had no secrets. But it's not true. Ivan has secrets from me, and I'm beginning to suspect they're big ones.

"I hate it!" I shout into the night.

"What do you hate?" Bea asks, but I don't answer.

"Come in. My parents are still at the party," Bea says when we reach her house.

"I think I'm going to head home," I say.

"Oh, come on," Katia says, but Bea laughs and says, "Yeah right, you're going home. You're going to go and get Ivan, aren't you?"

"Sure, Bea, I'm going to get Ivan."

Let them think what they want. I *am* going to get Ivan, but not for the reason they think.

*　*　*

I try texting him, but there's no answer. Not a surprise, because he always forgets to keep his phone charged. I also try the party, but Jack's mom says she saw him leave a few minutes ago.

I hardly ever take the road home from town because I love walking along the beach, but I have a better chance of finding Ivan if I go past his house, so that's what I do. I finally catch up with him as he's fumbling with the lock to his door. He opens the door and walks in, and I slip in beside him before he even notices I'm there.

"There you are," I say.

"Shit, Maddie, you scared the life out of me."

"I wanted to see if you were okay," I say.

"Okay as ever."

"You saved a girl from drowning this morning, remember?"

Ivan smiles at me and takes my hand. "You're my best cheerleader, Maddie."

"Want to come out to the beach for a bit?" I hold up the half-empty bottle of champagne that I'm still holding.

"Yeah, sure. I'll just get a sweater. Wait here."

Moonlight shines through the window at the top of the stairs and gives him a halo as he walks up. I haven't been up there for years. The last time must have been before Ivan's mom left. We used to have sleepovers, and I'm pretty sure the last time I went upstairs in Ivan's house was also the last time I had a sleepover with him. Ten, eleven years ago. It's not right that I never come here.

At the top of the stairs, Ivan stops abruptly, and I bump into him.

"What's that smell?" I ask.

"I don't know. You followed me?"

"It's like vomit," I say.

"Shit." Ivan's voice changes. "Shit, shit, shit."

The stench makes me gag when we open a door at the top of the stairs. Inside, Des lies on his bed. A gray-green ooze of vomit spreads from his beard and across his chest. His breathing is short and raspy; an old-fashioned alarm clock ticks by his pillow. When I step toward him, something crunches under my foot, and I look down to see broken glass and a smattering of pills strewn across the wooden floor.

"Oh, Ivan, what's he done?"

Ivan steps up to the bed and rolls Des over onto his side, then thumps him on the back until Des sputters and coughs. He groans loudly, and Ivan says, "Up, Des, get up."

Des groans again.

Ivan pulls the covers off Des and bends over so that his head and shoulders are under Des's arm, then pulls Des to a sitting position.

"Come on, Des, we're getting you into the shower."

Des opens his eyes and stares at Ivan. He tries to say something, but Ivan says, "Come on, Des."

My hands shake badly as I open the door wider so that Ivan and Des can pass through and stagger to the bathroom. The smell of alcohol trails after them, and the only sound I can hear is Ivan huffing as he mostly carries Des down the hall. My own breath comes out in gasps.

When they reach the bathroom, Ivan crouches down next to Des in front of the toilet and holds his head while he sticks his fingers down Des's throat. Des gags and retches, and again the stench of vomit stings my eyes. When he's done, Des leans back against the wall, but Ivan pulls him to his feet and into the shower.

I go back to the bedroom, where I use a slipper to sweep the broken glass into a corner. Then I pick up all the pills and pile them into the palm of my hand. There's no sign of a bottle they might have come from. I try to count the pills, but my eyes are blurred with tears, and in the end I just throw them into the pile with the broken glass.

The shower turns off and there's noise from the bathroom, but when I go out to the hallway, Ivan closes the bathroom door.

"Ivan?" I call through the door.

"We're fine," he calls back.

"Come on, open up," I say, but a second later he opens the door and steps out into the hallway, closing the door behind him. He's soaked, and his eyes are rimmed with red.

"Should I call an ambulance?"

He shakes his head. "He'll be fine."

"There were pills."

"I know. He's fine."

"But...Ivan..." My voice trails off because I can't find the words to say what I want to say.

There's more noise inside the bathroom, and then the door opens and Des lurches out. He's naked and still dripping from the shower, and when he sees me he stops and puts his hand out to steady himself, but when he does, he misses the wall and instead falls into Ivan, who stumbles and then falls, hitting his face on the doorjamb as he goes down.

I gasp and scramble over to cradle Ivan's head in my hands.

"Just go, Maddie," he whispers.

"What?"

He holds his head in his hands but sits up and says, "Maddie, leave."

"Maddie, leave," mimics Des. His words slur, and he stumbles as he rights himself.

I'm shaking so much I can hardly form the words to say, "No, I can't leave you."

"We're fine," Ivan says. He wriggles until he's untangled from Des and stands up.

"Come on, Des, into bed with you." He once again ducks under Des's arm and hoists him by the shoulder.

"Ivan." I reach out to him, but he moves away. "Please, Ivan, let me call an ambulance. Or Bo—let me call Bo. He'll come and deal with this."

"Just go, Maddie. We'll be fine." He turns his back to me and walks down the hall to another bedroom.

"Ivan!"

I follow him, but he turns at the door and says, "I know what I'm doing. You should just go." His voice is barely a whisper, but there's no mistaking that he means it.

I don't understand. Not at all. The only thing I want at this moment is to get Ivan some help, but he's already turning away from me again, and as he does, he says, "Please don't tell anyone, Maddie. Not Bo, not anyone."

He doesn't look back as he walks into the room and closes the door, and I don't follow him. I wait until I hear the sound of the two of them talking, and I can tell myself that at least Des is conscious now, and then I stumble down the stairs and sprint out the door as my eyes fill with tears. My breath is so sharp it hurts my throat, and my mind fills with the sound of Ivan's voice—the edge of panic, the desperate pleading. *Keep our secret*, he was saying. *Keep our secret like I always have.*

FIFTEEN

Ivan

Shit. How could I let this happen? After all this time, why the hell did I believe him? Why did I think if he said he would be away for the night that he would really be away? How stupid am I that I keep believing him?

My head spins as I stand up, but I've done this before, settled Des into my own bed, then crawled to the sofa and slept there for the night. We keep a blanket down here. I reach around in the dark until I find it, then pull it over me. My head throbs, especially my jaw.

I go in and out of sleep, but the throbbing of my jaw is constant. It's dark in here, and it stinks. My jaw needs ice. I wake up properly and wipe the drool off my chin and sit up, though my head pounds when I do so. This one's going to hurt for a long time.

There's movement upstairs, so I go up to check on Des. The blankets have slipped off him, so I cover him again, and I also close the blind, which I forgot to do earlier. What a fucking stereotype he is. At the door I hesitate until I hear Des start to snore, and then I head back downstairs and get an ice pack from the freezer. I close the door slowly and grab a dishtowel to wrap the ice in before I creep back to the sofa. My jaw hurts way too much for me to cry.

* * *

In the morning, Maddie's and Noah's voices outside wake me up.

"Ivan, wake up. Riley Point's going off. We're leaving in ten minutes with or without you," Noah says.

I roll over, but Noah calls again, "Ivan, we're coming in," and then both he and Maddie giggle, like they've got a shared secret.

Shit.

I roll over but don't get up until the voices get closer. When I hear the door open, I swing my legs over the edge of the sofa and sit up. The world spins, and I put my hands out to steady myself.

"You look like crap," Noah says, coming into the doorway of the living room.

I stare at the floor.

"Someone broke something last night. There's glass all over the kitchen floor," Maddie says.

I nod but don't say anything. Maddie joins Noah in the doorway. I breathe deeply. Count to ten, then look, I think, but before I can, she walks to the sofa, sits down next to me and puts her arms around me.

"Get dressed. We'll wait for you," she says. I still don't look at her face. My jaw hurts, but it's not too bad now, so I head upstairs to take a look at Des and get some fresh clothes. Des is snoring loudly. It stinks up here, but I'll deal with that later.

When I come downstairs a few minutes later, Maddie and Noah are picking pieces of glass up off the kitchen floor. It's a disaster in there—broken plates and glasses, food spilled all over the table.

"Leave it," I say.

"You guys really need to take better care of yourselves, you know," Maddie says. "Just because there aren't any women around here is no excuse for living like slobs."

"I know," I say.

"What happened to you?" Noah asks, pointing to my swollen jaw.

"You must have hit harder than we thought when you fell last night," Maddie says.

"I guess," I say. We look at each other, and her face tells me everything I need to know. She's not smiling, not frowning, just looking serious, like there's business to get on with today. No change from the way she looked at me yesterday. It's a totally Maddie look, and holy shit, I love her for it. I breathe properly for the first time since last night.

She takes my hand and wraps her fingers around it, then pulls at my arm so I have to follow her.

"So what's going on anyway?" says Noah.

"That is none of your business," says Maddie, but she smiles as she says it, so Noah laughs and says, "Well, it's about time. You two have been drooling over each other ever since I met you."

Let him think that if he wants. I don't care. I squeeze Maddie's fingers and follow her to the driveway, where River and Jack are sitting in Jack's car.

"Ready?" says Jack.

"Yep," says Maddie.

Jack looks at my face and shakes his head. "Ouch. What happened to you?"

"I fell."

"Looks bad," says Jack.

Maddie and Noah and I climb in the back, and Jack pulls away. Maddie sits in the middle and tells Noah about Riley Point. She shows him landmarks as we drive and laughs when he tells her a story about his sister.

But she holds on tight to my hand, and I hold on tight to hers.

SIXTEEN

Maddie

Surfing seems to help. I thought Ivan would sit out because of his swollen jaw, but instead he dives right in with the rest of us. He's on fire today. He catches everything and rides the waves like a dolphin. Graceful. Easy. How on earth did he ever convince us he was clumsy? Now that I've seen where the bruises come from, I can hardly believe I ever thought he just bumped into things.

The sight of Des falling into Ivan and Ivan hitting the doorjamb on his way down plays in front of my eyes all morning. It's only when I'm in the thick of the white water that it goes away, so I catch everything I can. It's the only way I make it through the day. The only thing that makes me forget I walked away.

We surf until the tide takes the waves away from us. As I pull my board to shore, Ivan rides up beside me.

"Maddie…" He pauses. We're alone in the shallows. The others are on the beach already, pulling off their wet suits. "Thank you," he says.

"For what?" I don't think my actions last night are anything to thank me for.

"For not saying anything."

"I'm not sure," I say.

"What do you mean?"

I take a deep breath, because I know this is not what he wants to hear. "I'm not sure it was the right thing to do. You should tell someone. Get some help."

He doesn't answer. Instead, he picks up his board and walks up the beach.

"Ivan," I call after him, but he doesn't turn around or stop or anything.

Shit. The tears that have been threatening all day push at my eyes again.

I follow him to Jack's car. Noah is already out of his wet suit, standing by the hood in his towel, eating a bag of chips. Jack struggles to pull his legs out of his wet suit, and Ivan sits in the back seat and blows on his fingers to warm them up. He doesn't look at me.

His face looks worse now that he's cold, the bruise a darker shade of purple. It breaks my heart to see it. How can someone so fit and strong-looking be so fragile?

I walk around to the far side of the car and yank at the zipper of my suit. My fingers are clumsy. I can't get it to move.

Noah comes over and says, "I'll do it."

I turn my back to him so he can pull on the zipper. He can't see my face that way either, can't see that I'm still fighting back tears. He gets the zipper down, then says, "What's up with Ivan? He looks terrible."

I don't know what to say, so I shrug and don't say anything. My voice might not work anyway if I tried. There's a towel in my bag, so I wipe my face and rub my hair with it. I hope Noah doesn't notice I'm stalling until my throat opens up again and I can speak normally. I take a deep breath to steady myself and say, "It was dark in his house and he tripped. It was bad."

Noah fingers his towel and frowns in a way that makes me wonder if he believes me, but I start pulling off my wet suit, so he goes back around to the other side of the car to give me some privacy. I sit in the front seat and hug myself to stop my body's shaking. I guess I'm keeping Ivan's secret. I guess I am.

When I'm changed, I fold my wet suit and roll up my towel, then gather my gloves and boots. There's a mesh bag I use to keep these all together when they're wet, but my fingers are trembling, and I can't open the bag. It snags and catches, and I can't get my stuff in. I can't see anymore anyway, because my eyes are blurry with tears, so I throw my gear on top of the bag and drop everything to the floor. Ivan finds me a minute later.

"Don't cry, Maddie," he says. He sits on the seat beside me. "I'm okay."

"But you're not. Des is not."

"We are."

How can he say that? His face is swollen. He is not okay. Looking at him puts my troubles with Peter in perspective. Ivan was right when he said I should be careful what I wished for, because this is what having a dad who doesn't care about you looks like.

"Come stay with us, Ivan. You shouldn't have to deal with this. Bo and Peter would understand. You know Bo already thinks of you as a son anyway. They love having you around."

The look on his face tells me I've made a mistake. Now it's him who has tears in his eyes, and he can hardly look at me.

"Maddie, I can't."

I shake my head but don't respond. He wipes his eyes with the back of his hand, then offers that hand to me. I take it, and the two of us sit together.

Once Jack and Noah finish dressing, Ivan and I shift to the back and let Jack drive us home. No one's talking much, but I notice that Noah keeps sneaking glances at Ivan. Maybe he suspects Ivan's bruise was more than an accident. I stare out the window so I don't catch his eye.

When we get back to town, Jack drives down the road where Ivan and I both live.

"Drop us at the path to Maddie's," Ivan says.

Jack slows down and pulls over so we can get out. Ivan and I gather up our stuff and wave goodbye to the others.

"What are you doing now?" Ivan asks as the car pulls away.

I think of all the things I'm supposed to be doing. Helping Noah's mom in her garden again. Helping Bo and Peter get the house ready for the Lazy Days party. Hanging with Katia. Painting. But I say, "Come with me. I want to show you something."

We leave our boards and suits on the rack at my place, and I lead Ivan down a path toward the headland.

"I haven't been out here for ages," he says.

"Almost there."

I'm pretty much the only person who ever uses this trail, so it's hard going, and we're splattered in mud before long. A mist fills the air, so the fir and spruce trees look ghostly as we pass beneath them. When we get to the headland, I stop and point up into one of the trees.

"What?" asks Ivan.

"In the tree, look."

I pull him around so he's standing in front of me, and I point so he looks in the right direction.

Without warning, a flash of black wings storms at us, flapping the air into tornadoes. We bend away, but they come back. Beak and claws and wings slash at our heads. We fling our arms over our heads and start to run. The raven caws after us, claws extended, pincers in the air.

"Keep running," says Ivan, and the two of us stumble back up the path. The bird follows, pecking at our arms until we reach the cover of a smaller tree and huddle under it. The raven perches above us, cawing madly, and we hunch together, panting and shaking.

"What the fuck?" shouts Ivan. He grabs a stick from the ground and waves it at the bird, but that just makes the bird angrier, and it lunges again.

"Be still. It'll think we've gone," I say. Ivan drops the stick and crouches deeper under the cover of the branches.

"Shit-crazy bird," he says.

"Shhh…"

We wait. Our breathing slows, and it's silent except for the hiss of drizzle on the branches and the creaks of the forest around us. Finally, the raven shuffles along the branch, opens its wings and flies away. We wait until it's out of sight before we leave the cover of the tree.

"What just happened?" asks Ivan.

"I have no idea." I'm shaking and cold. It's time to get out of this forest. We take the path back to the beach as quickly as the muddy, root-filled path will let us. We're both panting as we step onto the sand. When we leave the forest, we leave the mist behind us. The sky at the beach is a clear and open blue. Sun glints on the water. We both stop and breathe hard. I'm shaking, but it feels good to be out of the forest. A deep breath helps still my body.

"You were scared," says Ivan. His voice is teasing.

"You too."

"No I wasn't." He laughs as he says it because he knows he's lying.

"I think I need to sit here in the sun for a bit," I say. The stones near the shore are dry and hot, and their smoothness feels good against my legs.

"Lie back," says Ivan. He chooses a stone and places it on my arm. Its heat spreads across my skin.

"That feels great," I say.

Ivan finds another stone and puts it next to the first one, then another next to that, then another, until my arms and legs are outlined skeletons. The heat seeps into me, right to my bones, and for the first time all day my body stops shaking.

"Thank you," I say.

Ivan places one more stone in my hand and says, "Thank *you.*"

But he's wrong to say so. He's wrong.

SEVENTEEN

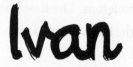

I manage to stay away from Des until late in the evening. When he sees me he winces, but he doesn't say anything, and neither do I. This is what I've learned. Stay silent. Don't remind him or he gets upset and does it again. When he finally does say something, it's just "I'm having a beer, want one?"

I shake my head. I'm in the middle of watching a bunch of old *Supernatural* episodes. I've seen them before, but it takes my mind off Maddie so I keep watching, but then Des sits down next to me and reaches for the remote to turn off the TV.

"I was watching that," I say.

"We need to talk."

I don't want to, but now that he's next to me I can tell he's sober, so probably it's okay. I shift to make room for him.

"I need some help," he says.

My heart jumps. I can't tell you how long I've been waiting to hear those words.

"I don't know if Pedro's up to the job, Ivan, and I really want this thing for the Salmon Festival to work. If I can start building again…" The sentence hangs, so I'm left to imagine the riches of our lives if Des can start building again.

"So I'm asking if you will step in, help me with the last of the building."

I stare at the screen, even though it's blank. Count to ten, I tell myself. Count to ten and let the disappointment slide away. Again.

At ten I turn to face him. "You should have asked me in the first place."

"Yeah, I know," he says.

Shit. So what do I do with that?

"Come on, buddy. We'll do it together."

I don't say anything.

"And I'll stay sober."

I shake my head. Heard that before.

"Seriously. I promise."

"The only thing that's going to make a difference is if you stay away from Pedro," I say.

"Yeah. I'll stay away from him. I promise. Come on, Ivan. This could be the change I need. And we could use the money. I haven't had many delivery shifts. And we're good together when we work, right? And as I say, no Pedro, and I'll stay sober."

"Okay," I say. "Okay." Because maybe, just maybe, he's right.

"Excellent," he says, pouring his beer out the window. "It'll be fun."

EIGHTEEN

Maddie

At home, I check into my henna supplies and look for more tattoo designs online. A few boys have started coming by asking for tattoos of dragons or swords or superheroes, which makes me wonder if Ivan showed his around on my behalf.

I should paint, but focus is not easy to come by today, and searching for images online doesn't take much concentration. Sitting on my bed with my computer seems like the right way to spend the evening.

After dinner, Peter comes to my room and asks me to help with something in the studio.

"Yeah, I'll come in a sec," I say. I've found a couple of images that might work, and I want to bookmark them so I can find them again to print them.

What seems like only a couple of seconds later, Peter's at my door again. "Maddie?"

"What?"

"Come now, please."

"Can't it wait?"

"I've been waiting. Now come on—I need you now."
Peter walks back into the hallway and adds, "Now, Maddie."

Out loud I say, "Jesus, Peter. One sec." Under my breath
I say, "Like there aren't more important things in life than
violins."

But maybe I speak louder than I think I do, because
Peter stomps back into my bedroom and looms over me.
He's almost shouting when he says, "That is enough, Maddie.
Your attitude sucks, you know. There are so many kids your
age who would give their eyeteeth to be you. Do you have
any idea how lucky you are to have talent and opportunity
and a family who's prepared to pay for your education?
Do you have any idea?"

I leap to my feet. "So what, you want me to bow down at
your feet and worship you for it? Thank you, Oh Generous
One." I hear my voice and can't believe these are the words
that are coming out of my mouth. I feel like I've been taken
over by some other person, a rude, nasty, spiteful person
who's saying things I don't even mean.

Peter's voice turns frosty. "You may not want to go to university, Maddie, but that doesn't mean you have to be horrible."

"It's all you ever talk about. Emily Carr University.
There are so many other things out there, Peter. So much
going on in the world. So many things to learn about and
to see. I just don't want to go, can't you understand that?

IDON'TWANTTOGO!" I screech so loud my voice cracks, and behind it tears and sobs flood into its place.

Peter doesn't move, but I sink to my knees and sob into my hands. He stands over me, silent, for a long time.

"Fine," he says at last. "I'll stop talking about it. It's your life, after all."

I don't look up until long after he's gone.

It wasn't even about university or about him.

NINETEEN

Ivan

In the morning Des and I drive to town, even though it's only a ten-minute walk—we have a lot of wood and tools in the van. I'm relieved to see Bo waiting for us outside the library door.

"I'm glad you're working on this too, Ivan," he says. There's no hint of anything in his voice, and I smile at the thought that Maddie hasn't said anything to him. He walks us over to where the stage is going to be set up and we sort out what needs to be done, and then Des and I spend most of the day working. Des was right—it is good when we work together. Des is still the best there is when it comes to wood and tools. The man can build anything.

I'm just getting to that achy stage where my body starts asking me about Jack's hot tub and how soon it can sink into it when Des stops and says, "I need food."

We both put down our drills and stretch. My back feels like someone stomped on it.

"I'll go get us some fish and chips," says Des. This is the second time lately he's offered to pay for food.

I lie down on one of the struts of wood. It's sunny for once, and the air is warm, so I close my eyes and let my skin soak it up. Sometime later Bo's voice wakes me. "You know, I could have sworn the stage was going to be bigger than this."

I sit up and peer at him. He's standing at the corner of the stage, looking at it, his hand on his chin.

"Really?"

"It looks small," he says.

"Does it?"

He nods. I get up and stand next to him. "How big were you expecting?" I ask.

"Twelve feet by twelve feet," he says.

It's not. A quick glance tells me that. I'd say more like ten by ten.

"Is twelve by twelve what you asked Des for?" I ask.

"I'm pretty sure I did," says Bo.

"Okay, well, I'll figure it out."

Bo smiles and pats me on the shoulder. "I know," he says.

When he walks away, I sit on the edge of the stage and think. Des comes back a couple of minutes later with fish and chips for both of us, and I say, "The stage is supposed to be twelve by twelve."

"No," he says, stuffing a bite of fish into his mouth.

"Let's see the notes Bo gave you."

"He said ten by ten."

"Let me see."

He grunts but digs in his pocket and pulls out his phone, then finds the notes and hands them to me.

"Twelve by twelve," I say.

"Shit, give me that," he says, grabbing the phone back from me.

"Shit," he says.

We both take a few bites of fish and chips in silence.

"We'll build the extra two feet separately and attach them," I say.

"We'll have to," says Des.

"You're welcome," I say.

We continue with our work, and when Bo comes by again, Des says, "The extra two feet are coming later."

Bo frowns and scratches his neck.

"We built it that way in case the stage has to get moved at the last minute to a smaller spot. It happens more than you'd think," I say.

"Ah," says Bo. "Clever thinking."

He watches us for a while, then heads off around the library.

We work for another half an hour or so, and then Pedro arrives.

"Fuck," I say under my breath when he turns from the sidewalk and comes toward us.

"Hey," Pedro calls.

Des puts down his drill and walks to meet him. They talk for a second, and then Pedro waves at me and leaves.

I could go home. I could go surfing. I could find someone to shout at, but instead I say, "I thought you said no more Pedro."

"I just have a couple of things to work out with him."

"That wasn't the deal, Des. Shit. That wasn't the deal."

He picks up his drill and bends over his work. Conversation over.

I get back to work too. We work around each other for a while. I don't say anything, but twice I almost throw down my drill and march down the street to find Pedro. Not that I can't guess what the couple of things are. Something to do with selling weed, or settling a drinking debt. What else would it be? Fucking Des. The more I think about it, the madder I get, until finally I can't keep quiet anymore.

"You promised, Des."

I say it softly, but Des hears. He stands up and turns off his drill. For a second I think he's going to throw the drill at me, but instead he says, "You still don't trust me, do you?"

"I'm trying," I say, gesturing to the stage.

"I'm just finishing up some business with Pedro, that's all."

"He'll screw you over, you know that?"

"You're so suspicious, Ivan. It'll be fine; we've got a plan."

"Yeah right. Look what happened last time I believed you," I say.

With that he pulls the bit out of the drill and puts them both down. Then he walks to the van, gets in and drives away. I get back to work, because if I don't have something to focus on, I'll scream.

* * *

Des eventually comes back to help finish the stage. We don't talk for the rest of the day, and when we're done, I throw my tools into the back of the van and say, "I'm going to Jack's."

Des nods and climbs into the van. As he drives away, I head to Jack's house.

Noah's already there, so the three of us sink into the hot tub and stare at the sky for a while. Jack's mom is in the kitchen, clattering dishes; his sister is in her bedroom, playing her flute; and his dad, Arne, is doing something in the garden behind us. Kyra stops playing flute and goes into the kitchen to talk to her mom. It's always so peaceful coming to Jack's house—everyone seems to like each other. Arne stops gardening and joins us in the hot tub, so now there are four of us sitting staring at the sky. We don't talk. We just soak. I could stay here forever.

"Dinner," calls Jack's mom.

"You boys joining us?" asks Arne, but Noah is expected at home, and I'm not up to sitting at the dinner table, so we get out with them and dry off. When they go into the house, Noah and I walk across the lawn to the road.

After I say goodbye to Noah, I head for home, but when I get to the bay, I take the path down to the beach and walk along to Maddie's house. Bo and Peter are on the deck with drinks and binoculars. I'm not sure I'm in the mood for them, but before I can turn around and pretend I'm not there, Bo sees me and calls out, "Ivan, come join us."

"What are you looking at?" I ask as I climb over the railing and sit down next to Bo.

Peter hands me his binoculars. "Grays or humpbacks—we're waiting for them to come a little closer before we decide."

I adjust the binoculars and stare out at the water. Looking for whales through binoculars is difficult, since you never know where they will come up, but I'm lucky, because I soon see a spout of water, followed by another.

"Two of them," I say.

"We think there are three," says Peter as he takes the binoculars from me.

"Is Maddie here?" I ask.

"She's gone to Victoria for a couple of days," says Bo. He takes a sip of his drink, then says, "Peter, how about a top-up."

Peter asks, "Ivan?"

"No, thanks," I say.

When Peter leaves, Bo says, "Ivan, I think you know what's happened to Maddie." He stares at me in a way that is just like Maddie's. His eyes pierce right through me, and I feel my face redden. "Look, Ivan, I don't know what's happening between you two, but I have eyes, you know, and I see things, and the truth is, I've been wanting to talk to you for a while."

There's a noise from the ocean, and he grabs the binoculars and looks through them for a minute. "Still too far away to tell." He puts the binoculars down. "How's Des?" he asks.

I shrug, which is what I always do when someone asks me about Des. "Same as usual."

"Our house will always be open to you, Ivan," he says.

I nod and I look away so he doesn't see the tears in my eyes. Shit.

"What did Maddie say?" I ask.

"She didn't say anything. Peter's cut up because he thinks it has to do with how much he's been pressuring her to go to Emily Carr. They had a big fight before she left, and he thinks he's driven her away, but I think it's something else. Something she doesn't know how to deal with. I think she's gone away to sort something out. What do you think?"

I take a deep breath and exhale slowly. There's nothing I'd like more than to tell Bo exactly what's going on. What's always been going on. But I don't, because much as I like Bo, I can't help but wonder why he's never asked more questions. Have I really been so good at hiding what goes on with Des? How hard it is for Des to keep it together? Des is an expert at looking good in front of other people, but still. Bo is a smart guy, and he notices things. So if he knows what Des is like, how come he's never done anything about it?

I turn away from him and look out to sea. One of the whales breaches just off the point, and Bo and I say, "Grays" at the same time. I don't want to think bad thoughts about Bo. He's a good guy, and I've known him all my life, but still, instead of answering his question, I ask, "Who'd Maddie go with?"

"She's visiting my sister, Alex. It's been a while since they saw each other."

"When is she coming back?"

"I'm not sure," says Bo.

Peter comes back out with their drinks, and Bo and I stop talking. We all sit there, waiting for the grays to come closer, but I can feel Bo's eyes on me, and I know he'll be watching.

TWENTY

Maddie

There are many things I don't understand. Chief among them is why. Why does Ivan stay with Des? Why?

The bus ride to Victoria is long and dark and rainy, just like my mood, and though I feel a little carsick by the end, I'm not ready to climb down the steps and into my aunt's arms.

"Maddie," she says with a smile. She holds me at arms' length and says, "Something's troubling you." Which is when I burst into tears.

"I see." She leads me to her car, and we drive for a few minutes until we reach her house. There are kayaks in the driveway, as always, and her garden looks like it's trying to escape. I love coming here. Inside, she brews a pot of tea and leads me to the back garden. Her little dog, Tintin, jumps all over me as I sit down on a blue plastic chair.

"Thanks, Aunt Alex, and thanks for letting me come here." The tea is hot and soothes my upset stomach.

"Is it about Peter?" Alex and Bo are close. He's probably told her all about my screaming session with Peter yesterday.

I shake my head. "Peter and I had a fight, but no, it's not about him."

"An affair of the heart?" she asks, which makes me laugh and spill hot tea on my shirt.

"Sort of," I say.

"Will you tell me his name? It is a him?"

I smile at her and say, "Yes, his name is Ivan."

"Ah, Ivan," she says.

"You remember him?"

"Of course. He has a beautiful smile, just like his father."

Oh my god, I've never thought of that. Des and Ivan are dissimilar in so many ways that I never stopped to think about it, but it's true they do look alike. Same build, same basic face shape, even some of the same gestures. But not the smile. Ivan's smile is so sweet.

"So..." says Alex.

I put down my teacup. A honeysuckle tendril waves next to my face in the breeze. I pull the stamen out and suck on it.

"The truth is, Aunt Alex, I can't talk about it."

She leans back and contemplates me. Her fingers play in Tintin's fur. "So you've come here to get away from something, to think about it for a day or two, but not to talk about it?"

"Yes, kind of." I don't want to be rude, but also I don't want to talk about it.

"I've set up your old easel in the spare room—it has the best light," Alex says.

"You're the best, Aunt Alex." I lean forward and give her a hug.

"I'll be here if you need me," she says.

The afternoon light is good in Alex's spare room, so I spend the next while sketching. I've brought pencils and paper with me, so I don't need the easel, but I use it anyway, because it reminds me of when I was little. The first thing I do is sketch Ivan, his anger bursting out of him. Then I draw him battling that anger with a sword that ends up looking more like a surfboard. Then I draw one of him and me, only he's pushing me away, and I'm pulling at him. Bo, Peter, Jack, River, Bea and Katia—they're all there too, sitting on the sides, watching. Watching and seeing. Seeing, but not really seeing. Isn't that what we've been doing? Watching but not seeing? My pencil strokes get thicker and darker as I go, until they're so damn heavy they tear through the paper. How could we, all of us, how could we watch and not see? How can it be?

My eyes are so blurred by tears I can't see my paper anymore, but it's just a scribble of black lines anyway, so I tear it off the easel and shred it into tiny pieces. I'm exhausted. Shit, I'm exhausted, so I lie on the bed and cry myself to sleep.

Alex wakes me sometime later by lying down beside me and saying, "Maddie, you've been crying for hours. Stop now. Tell me what's upset you this much."

"I can't. I promised I wouldn't," I say, sniffling. My eyes hurt, and my face feels swollen.

Alex sits up and leans against the wall. "Okay, here's the deal. You tell me, and I swear to God and all the goddesses and the nymphs and muses that I will evacuate whatever you say from my brain and never, ever tell a soul."

"You have a Pensieve? I've wanted one of those ever since I read Harry Potter," I say.

"I do."

I close my eyes and think for a second, then say, "What would you do if you knew someone was in trouble, but they made you promise not to say anything to anyone about it?"

"What kind of trouble? Financial? Emotional? Physical?"

"Maybe all of those?"

"Life-threatening?"

"I don't know."

Alex pulls herself up straighter against the wall. "He asked you not to tell anyone? Not Bo or Peter?"

"Not anyone."

Alex reaches over and straightens a strand of my hair. "And, Maddie, you think that's the wrong thing to do, don't you?"

I nod, and the tears start again. I don't do anything to stop them.

"But you don't want to betray him, am I right?"

I nod again.

"Well, Maddie, I think you have to decide what betrayal means," she says.

Which is exactly what I am afraid of.

"What would you do?" I ask. I love my aunt Alex. Today I'll do whatever she tells me.

"I had a boy here once. He had a very bad relationship with his mom, so he came to stay here with me for a while. It was good—they needed a break from each other."

"He liked being here?"

"Yeah, I think he did."

"What happened?"

"He eventually got a job and had a bit of money. I helped him find a place of his own."

"Did he ask for help? In the first place, I mean?"

"No. He was here one day visiting, and his mom came, and they ended up in a shouting match, and he just stayed, and after that I asked him if he wanted to stay with me for a while, and he said he did. His mother wasn't happy, but it was what was best for him."

"But it wasn't a hard decision for you?"

"No, Maddie, I didn't even think about it. It was what he needed." She shuffles across the bed and gets up. "I'll leave you, Maddie. I'll let you know when dinner's ready."

"Thanks, Aunt Alex," I say through my tears.

She bends to pick up the shreds of paper on her way out, but then straightens and leaves them there. "Maybe you want these," she says.

But I don't. I don't want any of it.

TWENTY-ONE

Ivan

Me and Des have been getting along okay in the couple of weeks since we got the stage built. It's always like this. Something shitty happens to him, he makes a mess of things by drinking too much, and sometimes, like this time, he goes too far, and I have to take care of him. When he's somewhat better, we fight for a while, he feels guilty and tries to make it up to me, we get along for a while, and then it starts all over again. That's been the pattern between us since I can remember. Well, since my mom left, I guess.

So now the festival has started, and all the people you never see from month to month because they're too weird for normal day-to-day life have come out of the woods and are crawling around the town. Anyway, they blend right in with the rest of the hippies and potheads around here.

I have to admit, Des has been working hard, doing odd jobs for Bo and the other festival organizers. He seems happy too. He even gave me money for groceries, and one morning he woke me up by vacuuming. True to his word, he hasn't been drinking, and I haven't seen Pedro all week. When Des doesn't drink, he doesn't smoke, so there's that worry gone too.

We both got up early this morning, and we're ready to go when Bo, Peter and Bo's sister, Alex, walk up the gravel road.

"Ready?" asks Bo, and I smile when Maddie appears from behind Peter. It seems like ages since I last saw her.

"You're back!"

"Came home yesterday. I wanted to be here for the Salmon Festival."

Town's already hopping when we get there. Maddie heads off to set up her henna booth, and Des and I follow Bo to the music stage.

"Looks great," I say to Des. The green room has been set up on one side of the stage and a sound booth on the other.

"You like the flowers?" Pots of bright red flowers are lined up along the front of the stage.

A handful of kids are running across the wood, sliding to the edge and laughing wildly.

"Does that look safe to you?" says Bo.

"Hey, kids, quit it," says Des. The kids stop and pout, but they get off the stage and run toward the market.

Bo laughs. "Okay, let's get to work."

There's a lot to do, getting the speakers and cords on the stage and setting up the sound system, but it's okay. Des and Bo talk about the festivals that were around when they were kids, which is sort of interesting. I never think about the two of them as kids. Bo must be older than Des, but they both grew up here.

"When did you come back, Bo?" I ask. I know he went away to university and even spent a few years teaching at the University of Toronto before deciding to go freelance.

"When we got Maddie. Peter and I didn't want to raise a baby in Toronto, and I thought Bear Harbour would be perfect."

"What did Peter think?" I ask.

Bo laughs. "Peter thought we'd arrived at the end of the world. It's a far cry from Stockholm or Toronto."

"So why'd you stay?"

"Maddie was about one at the time, and one day about three weeks after we arrived, we were down on the beach. She was just starting to walk, and she was toddling along the beach with Peter in tow. Peter got distracted by something and looked away, and in seconds Maddie was knee-deep in a pile of seaweed, with a batch of it in her mouth. It seemed okay, but then the next day she got sick, and we didn't know what to do, so I took her up the hill to your mom, and she told us that we had to take her to the clinic. Peter was all freaked out, and so was I, to tell the truth, but your mom drove us all to the clinic, and they gave Maddie some antibiotics."

He stops speaking, and I say, "That sounds like it would make Peter hate it here even more."

"At first it did," says Bo, "but then that afternoon your mom came by to see how Maddie was doing, and to bring some food over, and by the end of the week he'd met everyone in town. People brought us food and offered to babysit, and some women invited us to join their baby group, and Des and Arne told Peter they'd teach him how to surf, if you can imagine."

"Did he try it?" It's hard to imagine Peter surfing, but then, this was almost twenty years ago.

"He did," says Des. "He didn't like it. He liked fishing though."

I picture Des and Peter out on a fishing boat. I wish I'd known that Des. And that version of my mother too.

"So Peter decided he liked it here," I say.

"He did," Bo says. "Life in the city was always hard for Peter. Being here helped him forget some of those hard times."

"Remember when Ivan and Maddie both got the chicken pox?" asks Des.

He and Bo laugh, and Bo says, "Peter had the funniest remedies that he said came from his mother in Stockholm. He had the two of you smothered in porridge, but Des here didn't cool yours down, so he almost smothered you in hot porridge. Peter freaked out on him and yanked the clumps of porridge off. Des was so mad at Peter for not explaining properly."

I remember that. We must have been about eight. I still remember the feeling of the porridge sticking to me in warm clumps.

Bo and Des keep working, but I sit down on the edge of the stage. It makes me sad, thinking of how Des used to be.

"Come on, Ivan," says Bo, and the three of us carry another huge speaker from a truck onto the stage.

"That's it," says Bo once we've placed the speaker and all the other electronic equipment on the stage. "Thanks for your help, Ivan."

I leave Bo and Des talking about some last-minute details and go looking for Maddie. She's set up her stall with the colorful cloths, and already there's a row of girls waiting.

"Looks great, Maddie," I say.

She smiles at me, but then shifts her attention to a small girl pointing to one of the designs.

Maddie loves the market, but it's not really my idea of the best time, so I go in search of Jack or Noah or River. It's early still, but I'm pretty sure I'll find them where there's food, so I wander over toward the food court. I have to cross the park to get there, and as I go past the swings, Willow calls out to me, "Ivan, watch this."

"Buddy! How are you?" I say.

"Good. Look how high I can pump." She thrusts her legs back and forth until she's swinging way over my head, so high the swing misses a beat and jumps. She squeals, then laughs but slows down a bit.

"That's high, isn't it?" she says.

"Very high. Higher even than me."

She does it again.

"Where's your grandpa?" I ask.

Willow looks over her shoulder. "He went to talk to someone. He told me to stay here, but I'm hungry."

Yeah, typical. That's Pedro for you.

"You stay here and I'll go find him for you," I say.

"Bring me a Whale Tail," she shouts as I walk away.

"What do you say?"

"Puleeezzzz."

I laugh. "You got it, buddy."

I hum as I walk the rest of the way across the park and into the fringe of trees that circles it. The scents of freshly squeezed orange juice and something peanuty fill the air. This makes me hum louder. I love anything with peanuts in it.

As I come through the trees, I see Pedro and head toward him, but before I reach him, I see that he's talking to Des. Shit. Just when things were going well.

I can't hear what they're saying, so I walk in behind the public bathrooms and stand at the corner of the building, where I can see them but am partly hidden by the wall. I lean in closer, but the wall stops their voices from reaching me, so I walk behind a clump of trees where I can hear better. Pedro says, "Yeah, tonight. Around nine. I'll get you. He says it's good stuff."

I don't hear Des's response, but I do see him nod sharply, swivel and walk away. For a second I think about picking up a rock and throwing it at Pedro's forehead. What else can I do to get the guy out of our lives? It takes everything I've got to slow my breathing and count to ten. I'm about to walk away when I remember Willow, so I swallow hard and walk out from behind the trees.

Pedro's taken off across the field, moving way more quickly than I would have thought he could. I'm about to shout out to him, but instead I decide to follow him. He practically runs across the park to the street and heads out of town. As soon as he turns down the gravel road leading to my house, I know that's the only place he can be going. He's so determined to get there, he doesn't seem to notice that I'm behind him.

When we get to my house, he bangs on the door, and I almost shout at him, but then he opens the door and walks inside. I run up to the house and follow him in. He's not in the living room or the kitchen, so I run up the stairs to Des's room, but he's not there either. When I glance out the window, I see him skulking away, carrying one of the backpacks Des used to bring his weed to shore.

"Pedro," I shout from the bedroom window, but he doesn't look up or give any indication that he's heard me, so I run back down the stairs and out the front door. He's slowed a bit, so it only takes me a couple of seconds to catch up with him.

"Pedro." I want to lay into him so badly my hands have made themselves into fists, but instead I say, "What are you doing?"

"Just out for a walk," he says.

"Isn't that Des's pack?"

"He couldn't get away from the festival. Asked me to pick it up for him," Pedro says.

"What's in it?"

Pedro shrugs. "Stuff he needs for today, I guess." He adjusts the backpack on his shoulders.

"I could take it for you. I'm heading back there." My voice is a bit crackly, I'm having such a hard time not screaming at him.

"It's okay—I have to go get Willow," he says. He picks up his pace.

"Willow's hungry. She wants a Whale Tail," I say.

"Okay."

"She's waiting,"

"Oh, don't worry about Willow. She's a trouper," he says.

"Jesus, Pedro."

He turns away, and with that gesture he becomes an old man. Wrinkly. His fingers are gnarled. His beard is white, unkempt. Why am I afraid of this old man?

I follow Pedro from a distance to make sure he really does go back to Willow. He does, and when he reaches her, she leaps off the swing and launches herself into his arms. "I'm hungry, Grandpa."

"Let's go buy you a Whale Tail," Pedro says.

She grins. "Okay."

So trusting. God, so trusting.

TWENTY-TWO

Maddie

It's late in the morning, and my hand is tired from painting henna tattoos, when Ivan leans over my chair and says, "Will you come for a drive with me?"

"I wish I could," I say.

"You can."

"I promised Bo I'd help him get lunch ready. My aunt's in town, remember, and we're having a bunch of people over. Sorry, I'd rather spend the day with you, but I'm trying hard to get along with Peter, after that fight we had."

He frowns. "Ah. Peter."

"He can hardly even look at me, Ivan. I hate it. I feel like I'm walking on eggshells all the time."

"Yeah. I feel that way around Des most of the time."

I hardly know what to say to Ivan these days, but I still want to be with him as much as I can. If he's with me, he's not with Des, and that's got to be a good thing.

"Come with me. Come for lunch. Help me get ready. Come on, please." I smile at him, and he reluctantly smiles back.

"Okay."

He helps me pack up my stall, and we carry all my stuff home along the beach. Neither of us talks much. I know what I want to talk about, but I don't know how to get him to speak about it. He seems distant, distracted.

"Let's go sit at the water, just for a minute," Ivan says after we leave my market stuff in a pile on my bed. He reaches out his hand and takes mine. He seems pensive.

I follow him to the water's edge, where we stand, our feet on the damp sand.

"What is it, Ivan?"

"Nothing."

"You can tell me, you know," I say.

A dozen waves lap at our feet before he says, "Do you ever wonder, Maddie, what it all means?"

"Life?"

"Life."

Another dozen waves pass in front of us before I say, "Of course I do."

"Do you have any answers?"

I shuffle the sand with my feet. "Sometimes the waves talk to me."

It sounds stupid, and it's not something I'd admit to anyone but Ivan, but I have learned over the years that the ocean will answer many questions if you stand still long enough to listen.

"What kinds of things do they say?" Ivan's voice is teasing, but not in a bad way.

"That love makes us do stupid things sometimes."

Ivan takes his hand out of mine and steps away from me. "You're talking about me, aren't you?"

"I am." I can't tell if he's mad. He bends down and gathers a fistful of damp sand, which he clumps together and throws into the sea. Again he does it, and again.

"Shit, Maddie, I wish you'd never seen Des like that. I wish you were never there."

"I was though."

"Yeah."

Our silence beats around us.

"And I haven't said anything to anyone, like I promised."

"I know."

"And I'm here for you, if you need help."

"It's not like it happens often."

"You knew exactly what to do. You've been there before, many times. I could see that."

"It's okay though. We're fine mostly, and when we aren't, I can take care of it."

"It's not fine, and you shouldn't have to. Parents are supposed to take care of their kids, not the other way around."

There are tears in his eyes when he takes my hand. He doesn't say anything, but he runs his finger up the inside of my forearm, and I hear the waves sigh.

* * *

Bo calls us back to the house, so we join him and Peter and Aunt Alex, and we all get to work making lunch. Noah and his family arrive first, then Jack and his family. Katia and Bea come together, and finally River and his sister and their mom arrive. We all sit around on the deck and eat so much salmon and asparagus that there are only bones left and we're all practically moaning, we're so full. One by one, people get up and take their plates into the kitchen.

I love this time of year when the air off the ocean is warm, so I linger on the deck when I should be gathering dishes and helping Peter. Noah, River, Jack and Ivan start a stone-throwing contest. Laurie, Kyra and River's sister, Rain, go behind the house to see if any of the strawberries are ripe, though I've told them they aren't. The others are cleaning up, or else they've gone inside to look at Bo's collection of coastal art, so I'm left alone on the deck for a few minutes. The boys aren't far away; there's just a few stands of tall grass between us, so I watch them play. They're like kids, the way they jostle around on the beach, and Ivan's totally in there, though two hours ago he was serious, preoccupied. It's eerie, the way he makes himself look happy. How much of his life does he spend doing that?

What did he mean when he asked if I ever wondered what it was all about? Everybody does, so why ask? He seemed so serious, so wounded, like something else had happened, though I don't know what more can happen.

Even now, as he throws stones across the beach, there's something in the way he moves. Something extra. What I don't understand is why he keeps it all a secret. While I was in Victoria, I made an inventory of all the times Ivan's kept us away from his house or made excuses for Des's absence. We all bought into it. Every time. But why? Did we just not want to admit we knew something was wrong?

"The strawberries aren't ripe yet, but it looks like there's going to be a lot of them this year," Kyra says as the girls return from the back of the house.

"My mom says we can have some in our garden," says Laurie.

"I'll give you some strawberry babies," I tell her.

She grins at me and runs off to tell her mom, and the other girls follow.

A minute later they burst back out again with shoes and sweaters in hand.

"We're heading back to town. Fisher Boys are playing at four," says Kyra.

"You're coming too, right?" Laurie asks.

"In a bit," I say.

Jack's dad comes out and calls, "Jack, we're heading back. Ride with us?"

"I'm coming with River and Noah in a bit," he says.

Noah's mom asks Noah to help load up some lawn chairs she's borrowing for a party next week, and Bea and Katia want to stop at Katia's house to change into shorts.

River's dad suggests Peter and Alex walk with his family, and suddenly it's just me and Bo and Ivan standing on the deck.

"I think I need to lie down," says Bo with a yawn.

"Thanks for letting me stay for lunch, Bo," says Ivan.

"You are always welcome, Ivan. You don't need an invitation."

Ivan's face does a somersault as emotions crowd across it, but it lands back upright and he simply says, "Thanks."

* * *

Ivan and I walk back to the main stage in time for the afternoon concerts. He heads toward River and Jack, but I see Bea and Katia have already joined a couple of my friends from school who've come back for the festival. "Ivan, I'm going to sit with the girls."

He pulls on my arm, but I say, "Ivan, I'm tired of those guys. I'll see you later."

"I'll come with you then," he says.

"No. Go sit with your friends. I want to sit with mine."

Sally's seen me, and she's making her way through the crowd, waving and squealing, so I let go of Ivan's hand and say, "Go. I'll find you in a bit," and before Ivan has a chance to say anything, Sally engulfs me in a wild-hair-and-bangles hug.

It's good being with Sally and Astrid for a while. They're a year older than me and left for Vancouver the day after they graduated from high school, so seeing them today is special.

The music rocks, and the five of us dance until we're sweaty and thirsty and exhausted. Sally's a crazy girl—she moves like no one is watching and sways that wild hair and her big hips with abandon. I can't help but join in. The dance area is crowded. More and more people join us, and soon we're bumping into people as we dance. Astrid grabs my hand, and I take Sally's, and we form a chain that threads its way to the outer edges of the dancing crowd.

"I'm exhausted," says Astrid.

"I'm sweating like a pig," says Sally, lifting her hair off the back of her neck.

"Me too." My hair's in a braid, but still, it's hot, and I'm dying of thirst.

"I'll get us some drinks," says Sally.

"No, I'll go," I say. I don't tell them that I get this crazy fear in my chest whenever Ivan's out of my sight, and I need to go make sure he's okay.

I make my way to the beer garden slowly, to let the air cool me down and in hopes of seeing Ivan on my way. When I do find him, he's standing a bit apart from the crowd, and it seems that he's watching something. I follow his gaze, and I see Des talking with that old guy, Pedro. Des gesticulates like he's upset, and the other guy leans into him and points his finger right under his nose. Des storms off, and I look back at Ivan. He catches my eye, and we make our way to each other.

"What's up?" I ask.

He shrugs. "I got tired of listening to Noah bicker with Laurie and Jack take the piss out of River, and we were sitting too close to the speakers, so my ears are hurting."

I laugh. "Come sit with me and my friends."

"Nah." He shoves his hands into his pockets in a way that makes him look miserable.

"What's up, Ivan? You've seemed off all day."

He glances back toward where Des was talking to Pedro but doesn't answer me.

"Ivan?"

"I really don't want to talk about it, Maddie." His whole body retreats from me as he says this. He's shutting me out, so I try a different tactic.

"Do you want to get out of here?"

"And go where?"

"Earlier you asked me to go for a drive. We could go now."

"But you're having fun."

"I feel like a drive."

"Stay with your friends, Maddie. You should have some time with them. I'll come back in a bit."

"What are you going to do?"

"I'm going to check up on Des, you know."

"Be careful, Ivan."

"I know how to be careful, Maddie," he says, and I blush, because I realize it's true.

Before Ivan leaves, he takes my hand and says, "I'll see you later. Don't worry."

I'll try not to.

I'll try.

My friends have been joined by a bunch of other kids from school, so I spend the next several hours talking and laughing and dancing with friends. It feels good to laugh with them, but all evening long, part of me is waiting until later, until I'm back with Ivan.

TWENTY-THREE

Ivan

Des is gone. Packed his bags and left. He was here last night when I came in from the festival and checked on him. Drunk but snoring. But this morning there's a small pile of bills on the table, scrunched like they were pulled out of his pocket, held down by an empty mug. I open the fridge door for milk and see that he's taken the cooler and most of the groceries I bought yesterday. His coat is gone, and his boots, along with the jerry can he throws in the back of the van for long trips.

Upstairs, his bedroom looks the same as usual until I open the cupboard door and see that a bunch of his clothes are gone. His toothbrush isn't in the bathroom. Or his razor.

Well, shit.

I sit on his bed and look around. He's taken enough stuff for some time, more than an overnight, more than a couple of days. I kick at a pair of slippers half hidden under the bed and head back to the kitchen. Reaching for the money, I see a note among the bills and pick it up.

This should keep you for a few days. Love, Des.

He doesn't even say where he's gone or when he'll be back. I go upstairs and climb into bed.

I wake up later when my phone rings.

"What?" I say.

"It's me," says Des's voice.

"Where are you?"

"I'll be back in a few days. Did you get the money?"

"Yes. Where are you? What are you doing?"

"I'm on the road. I'll be back by Friday probably."

"But where are you? Are you on a job? What are you delivering?"

There's no answer, so I say, "You are on a job, right?"

"Yeah, on a job." I hear another voice, though I can't make out the words.

"Is that Pedro?" I ask.

He hangs up without answering.

Well, hell.

I throw my phone on the floor and pull the covers back over my head.

When it pings with a text later, I ignore it, and when there's banging on the front door, I ignore that too. Finally the sun goes down, and it's okay to be in bed, so I give in and stay there.

In the morning the sun shines through the window and wakes me up. I roll over and pull the pillow over my head, but the gnawing at my stomach is loud and painful, and if I don't pee, I'm going to explode.

Downstairs, the house is a complete mess. No wonder I stayed in bed all day yesterday. The sight of it makes me slump into the sofa. Shit. What am I supposed to do now? I run my hands though my hair and across my beard. It feels like days since I last washed. My teeth are fuzzy. My eyes hurt.

I rouse myself for a shower. Hot water feels good on my skin, washes away yesterday. Toothpaste. The best invention ever. I feel like new when I'm done, though my stomach still growls loudly. I even have energy to find a clean pair of jeans and a fresh shirt.

Bo catches me a few minutes later as I head into town to buy milk. "Ivan, you look terrible."

"I'm hungry." I don't know what made me say that, because I don't want Bo's help or Maddie's, for that matter, but maybe it's because I've eaten with them so many mornings over the years. Somehow I know he won't ask questions.

"Peter's making pancakes, I think," Bo says.

I take that as an invitation and follow him along the road toward the path down to his house.

Maddie and Peter have the table on the deck set with pancakes and syrup and steaming coffee already waiting and five plates, like they knew I was coming. My stomach growls loudly as I step onto the deck, and we all laugh.

"You'd better get started," Maddie says.

Nothing has ever tasted as good as these pancakes. I eat five of them before I even look up. When I do, Bo and Peter and Maddie and Alex are all staring at me.

"When was the last time you ate?" Peter says with a laugh.

I run the last piece of pancake through the syrup on my plate and shrug.

"When's Des coming back?" asks Bo.

It's hard to tell what he knows from the way he speaks, how he even knows Des is gone, so I simply say, "He'll be back by Friday."

"Where'd he go?" asks Peter.

"A delivery," I say. Maddie catches my eye, and we both look away quickly.

No one talks for a minute; then Peter says, "Maddie, pass the marmalade, please."

As she does, she says, "Ivan, want to come over to Noah's house with me today? I promised his mom I'd give her some more help with her garden."

"I thought about surfing," I say, though I'd mostly thought about spending the day in bed. I'm not sure I'm up for spending the day with Maddie.

"We can do both," she says.

"Well, I should probably also spend some time cleaning up my house. It's kind of a disaster."

"What did you do all day yesterday? I went looking for you," she says.

I shrug. "Spent the day in bed."

She pinches her lip with her teeth and creases her forehead, but doesn't say anything more.

Bo pushes back his chair and says, "I'm going to start building the new shed today. I was hoping you and Des would have time to help, Ivan, but I need to get some stuff organized first."

"I will, for sure, and Des, he will too, when he gets back," I say. Maddie stares at me but doesn't say anything.

"All right, then, let's get this day started," Bo says, and he and Peter and Alex all take their plates and head into the house. Maddie plops the second half of her last pancake onto my plate and holds up the syrup. "More?"

I nod. "Thanks, Maddie."

She smiles.

"I mean for not saying anything to Bo and Peter."

She leans over until I can't avoid looking her in the eye, then says, "I told you I wouldn't, didn't I?"

"But thank you anyway."

We both chew for a bit, and then she says, "They're not stupid, you know. They'll figure out that something's up."

It makes me laugh to hear that. How many years have I been living this life without anyone noticing? It's not me they're noticing; it's Maddie. They're tuned to her troubles, not mine. And I know I can't have it both ways: I can't tell everybody to butt out and also want them to help me.

"They both just shrugged off the fact that I said my house is a total disaster and I spent the entire day in bed yesterday and Des is not around to help with the shed."

Maddie's face puffs up and goes all blotchy, and her voice cracks as she says, "But Ivan, you work so hard at not letting anyone know what's going on with you. How could they?"

"Yeah. But still…"

"Sometimes you wish they did?"

"It's just…sometimes I wonder if I'm really that good at hiding things?"

Her eyes tear up as she says, "Yeah."

"Bo and Peter—and everyone else around here, including you—have ignored all kinds of things," I say. Even though I've just eaten a whole pile of delicious pancakes, I am still in a pissy mood.

"Yes," she says in a tiny voice. "I know."

TWENTY-FOUR

Maddie

The sky clouds over when Ivan says the words *including you*, and I shiver. How can he be so cruel?

He eats the last of the pancake, looks at me like he thinks I'm going to bite him, says, "I'm sorry" and leaves. I put my head down on the table and cry. Again. All I seem to be doing these days is crying.

A long walk along the beach helps clear my mind, solidify some ideas. I'm gone a long time, and when I get back, I head over to the studio.

"There you are. Can I talk to you for a sec? And Bo," I say.

"I'll be right in," Peter says.

Bo's in the living room at his desk. He's been working for hours on an article about the impact of sea-otter populations on kelp harvesting.

"Bo, I have something to tell you. Peter's on his way in."

He swivels around in his chair and pulls down his glasses. When Peter joins us a second later, I take a deep breath and say, "I've decided to go to Emily Carr."

"You have?" Bo asks.

"Yep. I have."

"It wasn't because I pressured you so hard, was it, Maddie? I'd feel bad if it was," Peter says, though I'm not sure I believe him.

"No, I decided it's the best thing to do after all, the best way to learn."

Peter and Bo both beam at me like I've just told them they've won the lottery. Peter reaches out and pulls me and Bo into a hug. "We'll have to let them know right away and sort out a residence."

"I'd like to live off campus," I say.

Peter opens his mouth to object. I know what he's going to say: Vancouver's a big, expensive city, and I don't know anyone there, and it's not safe, so I quickly add, "With Ivan."

"Ivan's going to Vancouver?"

"Yes." I haven't asked him yet, but I'm sure he will. Who wouldn't want to get away from the crazy situation he's in?

"That's good. We've been worried about him."

"How long have you known?"

"Known what?" Peter asks.

"That—" But then I think, What *do* they know? Maybe they don't know as much as they think they do. "That Des and Ivan need help."

"A long time, Maddie."

I sit with that for a minute, watching the dust motes swirl in the late-afternoon sun. The sense of relief I just felt is being replaced by something else, and it takes me a minute to understand that it's disappointment.

My voice is shaky when I say, "If you knew, how come you didn't do anything?"

Bo closes the lid of his computer and turns to me before he says, "Maddie, family troubles are hard to interfere with. Peter and I have always tried to support both Des and Ivan in any way we can." He sweeps his hand around the room, and my eye follows his arm. "Do you think we really need this much shelving? And I'm pretty sure either Peter or I could have cut all that wood last year. And our grocery bills would be a lot smaller if Ivan didn't eat with us so often. We've suggested Des get some professional help, but he always shrugs off the idea. Early on we debated getting social services involved, but we thought Ivan might be taken away, not just from Des, but from all of us. We decided the best thing to do was just keep an eye on them and help where we could."

We sit in silence for a long time while I think about what he's said. So they know at least some of what's going on. But do they know how much Ivan takes care of Des? How bad it gets?

* * *

Ivan acted like he didn't want to see me this morning, but I'm on a mission, and I won't give up.

I walk up the path just as he's coming the other way from the forest behind his house. His hair has sticks in it, and his pants have what looks like sawdust in a streak down the leg.

"What have you been up to?" I ask.

He shrugs his usual noncommittal shrug and tries to turn me down toward the beach, but I sidestep him and say, "Ivan, can we go inside? I want to talk."

"Let's go to the beach."

I know he wants to get me away from his house so I won't see the state it's in, but that's part of my plan, so I say, "Let me in. I really have to pee."

He frowns, and for a second I think he's going to tell me to pee in the woods, but then he reaches for the door and pushes it open.

It's worse than I thought it would be. Somehow I'd imagined what my house would be like if someone threw stuff around, but I'd forgotten to factor in the years of neglect Ivan's house has suffered. When I've been here recently, I've been so preoccupied by other things that I didn't really look around.

"You said it was a mess, but this is something else," I say. The garbage overflows the can, dirty dishes fill the sink and the smell of the unwashed dishes hangs in the air. "Jeez, Ivan."

He shrugs again. Super communicative today. He points down the hallway, and I pick my way past piles of stuff to the door. As soon as I open it, I regret it. The smell of mold hits me before the stink of dirty clothes, and whatever's stuck in the sink makes my stomach lurch. I pee as quickly as I can into the filthy toilet and make my way back to the living room, where Ivan has already picked up some of the papers lying around.

I take a good look around the room. When I was little, I used to come here sometimes with Peter. He and Ivan's mom were friends, and he'd bring me here to play when he came for coffee. I'm sure there were curtains on the windows then.

"You used to have curtains. White with yellow flowers," I say.

"Sunflowers. Yeah, we did."

"What happened to them?"

"That was years ago," says Ivan.

"When your mom was here."

He doesn't answer.

He never talks about his mom. Never. I always wondered about that, but one day when I asked why he never spoke about her, he said he tried writing to her when he was little, and she never responded. I can only imagine how much that would hurt.

There used to be framed pictures on the walls, bright, like the curtains, but now there are yellowing maps stuck into the plaster with thumbtacks.

"That's a lot of maps," I say.

"Charts," Ivan corrects me, and he's right. They're charts of the islands. Someone, probably Des, has made notes all over them.

"What are the red dots?"

"Red dots are creeks where the water's not brackish, blue are navigable beaches, yellow means there's usually surf, so coming off the beach can be tricky, and green shows hidden rocks."

"I'm impressed. You guys know a lot about the area. I bet Bo would love to see these."

I walk to the wall to look more closely, but Ivan takes my hand and says, "Let's get out of here."

"Wait. There's something I want to say."

He looks scared now as he waits for me to speak. I don't know how he'll react to my plan, so I just come out and say it. "Come to Vancouver with me."

The startled-deer look grows wilder, so I say, "I'll go to Emily Carr like everyone wants me to, and you can get a job or study or something. We can live together in a crappy apartment. It'll be so awesome—" I stop, because his face looks like he just heard someone he loves has died.

"It would just be for a little while, until Des sorts himself out. Then you could come back if you want."

Ivan stares at me, but his eyes are not seeing me at all. They're a thousand miles away, and I'm not even sure he's heard what I said.

"Say something." I reach out my hand, but he doesn't take it, so I grab his, and even then his hand is limp, like he doesn't realize I'm holding it.

"Is it because the house is such a mess?" he says.

"No, of course not. It's not that at all. Well, maybe a little bit."

"So…you've told Bo then. Or Peter."

It's terrible to look at the face of a person who thinks they've been betrayed. I pull my hand back, and my voice is barely a whisper when I say, "I haven't said anything they didn't already know."

"So what do they know?"

"That you and Des have difficulties. That's all—I swear."

He turns away then and walks out of the room. I want to follow. My whole body wants to follow, except my feet won't move. It is wrong. All wrong. And I don't know why. The house is a disaster, and so is Des. Ivan can't stay here—he can't. My feet finally unglue from the floor and allow me to follow him. He's at the sink, running water.

"I can tidy the house," he says, not looking up from the sink.

"Ivan…it's not the house…" I don't know what else to say.

"Just go, Maddie."

Again my feet stick to the floor as my mind scrambles around, looking for something to hold on to, some raft to cling to. But he turns the tap up so the water's loud, and he slams dishes back and forth. After watching him for a minute, I go.

This is the part I don't understand: why he will never leave.

TWENTY-FIVE

Ivan

Maddie thinks she can fix everything by getting me to move out. Like not being here would somehow make everything okay. Des would solve his problems and start a new life, and we'd have a great relationship. We'd be partners in a carpentry company. We'd build beautiful bed frames and doors and shelves, and we'd sip beer together while making jokes, and there'd always be money for groceries. He'd be good at taking care of himself, of staying out of trouble. On stormy days we'd spend hours surfing. Pedro would stop pressuring Des, and little Willow would grow up happy and free. Violins would sound. The sun would shine.

Nobody gets it at all. Not even Maddie. And if she doesn't get it, no one will.

The water in the sink is hot, but it cools fast as it lands on my shirt, and soon I'm standing at the sink shivering, so I take my shirt off and use it as a rag to wipe down the counters and cupboard doors. Once the doors are clean, I vacuum the floor, then take out the garbage and put a new bag in the garbage can. The place still smells of old food, so I root around in the recycling until I find a jar to rinse out, then reach out the window and pick a few tendrils of honeysuckle and put them in the jar.

I'm on a roll, so I clean up the living room, even dusting the windowsills and under the carpet. Then I gather the piles of newspaper stacked up on the dining-room table and throw them into a recycling bin. We don't own a tablecloth, so I make a mental note to buy one.

The worst is the bathroom, but I'm not about to stop now. It feels like it takes hours to scrub the walls and wash out the sink and the tub and the toilet, but it looks pretty good when it's done, and I add soap and new towels to my list.

Upstairs, I pull all the sheets off both beds and make them up new, then dust and vacuum and tidy until I'm so tired I'm dragging my butt around. When I'm done, I open the windows to let in some fresh air, and then I pull off the rest of my clothes and stand in the shower, letting the hot water steam away what's left of my anger.

Fuck Maddie and Bo and Peter. What gives them the right to try and run my life? How come they're never there when Des gets so drunk he can't take care of himself? Or when he loses yet another job? Or gets caught up with Pedro? Or spends days and days in bed not eating? Or almost burns the house down? They don't even know about that. I don't need their help. Never have. I'm not sure which is worse. No one knowing, or Maddie and her family interfering. Both feel shitty.

The water runs over me, down my shoulders and across my back. It feels good. When there's no more hot water, I turn off the tap and reach for a towel, but there isn't one. They're all sitting in a pile beside the washing machine. And there's no one for me to call to bring me one.

*   *   *

When Des finally returns at the end of the week, he finds the house clean and smelling good. There's toilet paper on the roll in the bathroom, soap at the sink and a tablecloth on the table.

"I guess you don't need me at all, do you?" he says as he slips off his boots in the mudroom. "Got groceries too?"

He's right. I don't need him. "There's a fridge full."

"And beer?"

"Fuck off."

He clenches his face tight and stops himself from hitting me. I can tell. I've seen the signs before. He's drunk, at least a little bit. He goes away, and when he returns he's drunk.

"I need a drink," he says, and he picks up his boot to pull back onto his foot.

"Whatever." I slip my flip-flops on and head out the door ahead of him.

* * *

I walk over to Jack's. Noah's already there, and the three of us take out longboards for a while, then soak in the hot tub. Jack's mom offers me dinner, and afterward Noah and I head to the beach for a while before it gets too dark. The surf's crap, but that's okay. We just sit on the sand and watch the waves come in.

I don't move when Jack walks down the beach toward us, though I'm surprised to see him.

"I thought your mom wanted you to stay home this evening," I say.

"You better come with me." His eyes slide over Noah, and he doesn't explain. There's something in his voice, a tightness that makes me sit up.

"What's happened?"

Jack's eyes slide over Noah again, and he doesn't say anything, so I say, "Just tell me."

"It's Des. He's been beaten up. Bad. You'd better come."

Noah and I follow Jack up the path to the road, where Jack starts walking fast. "I found him when I was on my way to visit my uncle," he says.

"Found him?" asks Noah.

Jack doesn't answer until we come to a bend in the road where the grass grows tall and an apple tree casts shadows on the ground. Des is sitting in the grass, covered in blood and vomit, groaning.

"He refused to come to the clinic or to let me help him," says Jack.

Des looks like he's had the shit beaten totally out of him. He looks up at me, and my gut clenches, because his eyes hardly see me at all.

"Des," I say as I lean over him. His breath stinks of alcohol, but I already knew it would.

"Shit," says Noah. His face has gone white, like he's never seen someone who's been beaten up before, which he probably hasn't.

"You get under his left arm," I say to Jack. I push my shoulder under Des's right arm while Jack gets under his left, and between the two of us we hoist him to standing. He drools onto my neck, but my arms are too busy holding him up to wipe it off.

Between the three of us, we half-lead, half-carry Des home. We drag him up the stairs to his room and let him flop onto the bed. Jack rolls him over so he's on his side, and I pull off his boots. When I stand up, my hands are shaking.

"Do you want us to stay?" Noah asks, but I shake my head. I don't even look at them as they leave.

I sit on the edge of Des's bed and listen to him snore. There's a little bird outside the window. A small brown one, and it picks away at something in the dirt. I've tried gardening out there, but nothing ever grows, and the ground's rock hard from years of neglect and from our hard work boots pounding on it. Nothing ever grows, and nothing ever changes. No matter how hard I try. Des snorts and rolls over. He's asleep, but his eyes are open, and he looks weird. The bird keeps pecking, but he's not getting anything. That hard earth won't give way. I know it. Des snorts again, and I get up and leave the room. In my own bedroom I glance out the window. The bird's still there, trying for a worm, as I pull off my boots and throw myself into my bed.

TWENTY-SIX

Maddie

Ivan's avoiding me. I haven't seen him for more than a week, and I don't know how to respond to that, so I decide the best thing is to go somewhere I know he will be—Jack's house.

It's late when I arrive, and I'm pretty sure the boys are drunk or on their way to being drunk when I come in, but they all scooch over on the sofa so there's a space next to Ivan, and he smiles up at me, so I slide in.

"What are you watching?"

"Something crappy," says Laurie, but she reaches across Noah and puts her hands in the popcorn bowl, then snuggles back down between her brother and Jack.

"It is crap," Ivan whispers in my ear. "Let's go." He stands and puts his hand out, so I take it.

"You just got here," says Laurie, but Noah says, "Shut up, Laurie," and they all laugh as we cross the room.

"Where are we going?" I ask.

Ivan is purposeful as he strides across the lawn. "The beach."

"It's so late. What're you thinking?"

"Just come."

We walk in silence down the street and along the path. It's still twilight, even though it's past ten. The sky is like ink, and the summer air is soft and still warm from the day.

"Let's stop here," says Ivan. He sits down with his back against a log and his legs straight out in front of him.

"What did you want to come here for?" I settle next to him, but when he doesn't answer, I turn to face him and see that he's looking at the ground.

Without looking up, he says, "I can't come and live with you, Maddie. I can't leave him alone, that's all. I just can't."

"But why? I mean, why don't you just phone someone? There must be someone who can help. Not the police— I don't mean that. A counselor, someone like that."

He laughs, but not because I'm being funny. "You're talking to someone who's spent his whole life trying to avoid counselors, youth programs, social services, all those people."

"Okay, so not a counselor. A friend? What about Peter and Bo? They would help, they really would. Please let me tell them, please."

He shakes his head.

"What are you afraid of, Ivan?"

"This was a mistake. Let's go. I'll walk you back to Jack's." He stands up and brushes the sand off his legs.

I follow him, but after a few steps I say, "I'm sorry. We'll do whatever you want. I promised I wouldn't tell, and I haven't. Let's sit again. Come on." I reach out to take his hand and pull him down next to me. "I don't want to go to Jack's. I only went there to find you," I say.

"You did?"

"Yeah," I say.

Though it was light when we got here, the stars are starting to show. Ivan shifts around until he's comfortable, and I curl up next to him, and we lie together, staring up at the pinpricks of light appearing across the sky. The sand is still warm from the sun, but it's cooling fast, so I wrap my feet around Ivan's legs to warm them. He puts his arm around me, and I snuggle my head against his chest. Ivan raises his hand and squints past it, so I do the same, blocking out the sky so I can look at the stars individually.

"What do you see?" I ask.

"Betelgeuse," he says.

"Silly. What do you really see?"

"Pluto."

"Come on."

He doesn't answer. Instead, he lets his hand drop back to his side. "Would you really go to Emily Carr just for me, Maddie?"

The question makes me laugh. My mind has been so far away from art school that I haven't had a moment to think about it, despite what I told Peter and Bo. But now, lying on the beach here, I know I can't go. How could I leave him now?

"I probably won't go," I say.

"You should."

"How do you know what I should do? You can't even figure out what to do yourself."

"If I had a talent like yours, I'd know."

"What do you think you'd do then?"

"I'd study my ass off until I was the best damn painter I could be, and then I'd paint the shit out of everything until I painted my way right out of here into a different life."

"So come to Vancouver with me. That's a different life."

"I can't."

Oh, Ivan. I hug him as tightly as my arms will let me. "We'll find a way. We will."

If only it didn't get cold at night, we could stay here together until tomorrow. But I'm already shivering despite being wrapped up in Ivan's arms and legs.

"We better go," he says at last, and we stand up and wipe the sand off ourselves, but when he turns to head to his house, I take his hand and pull him toward mine. We don't speak as we make our way around to the back of the house, and we're quiet as can be as we climb through my bedroom window and creep across the room, being careful not to make the floorboards creak. Ivan hesitates when I pull back the covers of my bed, but I don't want to let him out of my sight, so I keep hold of his hand as I climb in, and we fall asleep together. There's no way I'm letting him go.

TWENTY-SEVEN

Ivan

I wake up at dawn and climb back out of Maddie's bedroom window. Last thing in the world I need right now is for Bo or Peter to find me there. Even though we slept fully clothed, I can just imagine what they'd make of my being there.

Des comes into the kitchen and says, "Do we have milk?" He still has a black eye and looks terrible.

I open the fridge and point out the jug of milk in the door.

Des pours himself a glass, then says, "Lazy Days party tonight. You going?"

I nod. "Are you?"

"For sure. I thought I'd go down this afternoon and help Bo and Peter set up their tables."

"They're expecting me too," I say. No need for him to know I was with Maddie last night. Thank God he didn't leave any cigarettes burning or any bathroom taps on. My heart skips a beat thinking about it.

After we've both eaten and taken showers, Des and I head down the path to the beach and over to Maddie's place. The three of them are sitting on their deck, drinking coffee. Maddie stands up when we're still partway down the beach and walks into the house. When we arrive, she comes back out with two cups in her hands.

"One for you," she says to Des. "And one for you," she says to me.

I take the cup from her. I want to say thank you or something for last night, but there's too many people around, so I sit down without saying anything.

"Ouch," says Bo, pointing at Des's eye.

"Yeah, it hurts. Surfing accident," Des says.

The silence is uncomfortable. It seems impossible in this small town that anyone wouldn't know that Des was beat up last week. Even though I don't exactly know who did it, I can guess it had something to do with Pedro. But neither Bo nor Peter says anything. We all sit quietly for a few minutes and listen to the waves and the seagulls. Then Bo says, "What's the plan, Peter?"

Peter stands up and stretches. "I told Jason I'd come by and get their barbecue before ten, so I'd better get going."

"I've got the tabletops in the back of the van, Des, if you can help pull them out," says Bo.

"I've got the lanterns ready to put out, but I need help unraveling the flags," says Maddie.

I follow Maddie to the sheds at the back of the house. The wood for the new shed is still sitting there, waiting for us to get to it. Maddie pulls open the door of one of the other sheds and we go inside.

"Thanks for last night. It was nice—I mean, the beach and then sleeping in your bed with you. It was warm." That's the clumsiest-sounding thank-you a guy ever made, and she tilts her head for a second as if she's trying to understand what I'm saying.

Then she says, "Yeah, it was nice. You snore though."

* * *

It takes the whole morning to string the flags and set out the lanterns. People keep dropping by with extra plates or chairs or coolers, and by lunchtime there's already a bunch of us sitting around on the deck, drinking beer and eating food that was probably meant for the party.

Jack and Noah come by around two with salmon for the barbecue, their sisters trailing behind with badminton nets that they put up in the sand.

"Let's play," says Laurie, and she throws the birdie at me and Maddie, so Maddie and I play against Laurie and Kyra.

"You girls are pretty good at that," Maddie says.

Kyra laughs an evil laugh. "Oh yeah! We're the best."

"Either that or you two are drunk," says Laurie.

Maddie laughs. "There could be some of that too. Speaking of which, I need a drink. Anyone else thirsty?"

"I'd like something," says Kyra.

"I made a huge jug of lemonade," says Maddie.

We gather the birdie and the rackets and walk back up the beach to the house in time to see Des and Bo installing a keg.

"How'd you get that thing down here?" I ask.

"Don't ask," says Des.

"Who cares?" says Jack, who's already got a mason jar under the spigot.

By five the whole town is here, plus a whole lot of people from the islands nearby. The house is full of flowers and food and people. The table on the deck is overflowing with bowls and platters of food. The smell of barbecued salmon makes my mouth water.

"Grab us a place to sit, and I'll get plates," I say to Maddie.

I head to the food table. It's crowded, so I lean on the railing overlooking the water until a space opens and I can fill our plates. I search for her among the crowds of people sitting on logs and lawn chairs along the beach. The tide is low, and people are strewn in clumps way down the beach. She's with Peter, Des, Jack, Noah, Bea and Katia. I sit down, and Peter stands and says, "Des, let's leave these young folks alone," and the two of them laugh and walk away.

"No offense, but don't you guys find it weird that Des and Peter are friends? I mean, Peter's so..." Noah's voice trails off as Maddie stares at him.

"So what?" she says.

"Gentle," says Bea before Noah can answer. "And that's not a word I would use to describe Des. No offense, Ivan."

"Exactly," says Noah.

"Peter was good friends with Ivan's mom," says Maddie.

I know what's coming—some question about my mom that I don't want to answer. So I say, "There was one time, when I was about eleven or so, when a bunch of us hiked up Mount Arrowsmith for the weekend. Bo was there, I remember, and Jack and Arne and some other guys, and for some reason Des and Peter got left behind to put up the tents and build a fire and get some water boiling. I went off hiking with the other guys, and I remember that they were laughing about what shape Peter would be in when we all got back. But when we returned, they had all the tents up, coffee was already made, and Peter was sitting on a rock, whittling sticks for roasting hot dogs. Des and him have been friends ever since."

"I remember that," says Jack.

"I've been to Mount Arrowsmith too," says Katia. "It's magical. From one side you can look down and see across Georgia Strait to the lights of Vancouver, and if you look the other way you see the Pacific and the west coast."

"People misjudge Peter a lot," says Maddie.

"It was fun, that trip," says Jack. "Remember how Des taught you how to throw a line into a tree to make a food cache, Ivan?"

"Yeah," I say.

"He also taught us how to make a fishing line out of a stick and some grasses," Jack says.

"He did," I say.

"How come I wasn't there?" says Maddie.

"Guys only."

"Typical."

The conversation turns to camping and near misses with bears and whales, but I tune it out and think about that trip and how much fun me and Des used to have.

TWENTY-EIGHT

Maddie

Looking at Ivan's face as he tells Noah about the things he and Des used to do makes me want to cry. How dare he be that nostalgic? I stand up and head to the house just to get away from that look. There are people everywhere, so I toss my paper plate on the compost pile and walk through to my bedroom and close the door. The sounds of a guitar and a violin float in from outside; the air is soft tonight. I lie on my bed and take a deep breath. I always love the Lazy Days party, but tonight I'm distracted. To be honest, I spend most of my waking hours thinking about Ivan and what to do about him—I mean, how to help him.

I've learned something about Ivan tonight, listening to him talk about his dad and the things they used to do together. Des's total flakiness, his inability to take care of himself, all the crap he gives Ivan—the reason Ivan puts up with it all is that he remembers what Des was like before.

He remembers another life. I remember that time in our lives too, when Ivan was a kid and he used to run around after Des like a little shadow, always smaller, but always there. Des would come over to talk to Peter, and Ivan would be with him. I remember seeing Des and Ivan in town together, Ivan sitting in the passenger seat of Des's van while Des talked to his clients.

I guess what changed is that Ivan's mom left. Ivan was little then, and you'd think he was the one who suffered more, but maybe it explains a lot about Des. If you think about it that way, he's a man who is suffering. But the stuff he does still isn't okay. There's no excuse for making your kid your keeper, even when he's not a kid anymore. But maybe that's not the way Ivan sees it. I guess he thinks that the old Des, the one who used to have his kid with him all the time, is still in there.

I'd like to spend the rest of the evening lying here alone with my thoughts, but I'm supposed to be helping with the piñata. When I hear the kids running around outside my window, I get up and go out.

"Anyone for a piñata?" I ask.

About twenty kids of all ages jump up and down in answer, so I lead them to the side of the house where we hung the piñata earlier.

"Littlest first," I say, and the kids jostle around and then push a tiny kid, who must be only three or four, to the front.

"Have you ever hit a piñata before?" I ask.

He shakes his head, so I give him the baseball bat and place his hands on the handle. He can hardly hold it up.

"Watch out," I call to the other kids, motioning for them to stand back. I crouch down and wrap my arms around the little boy and help him hold on to the bat. "Ready?" I ask.

"Yes," he says, and together we swing at the piñata. It sways but doesn't break, and it's the next kid's turn.

The piñata lasts long enough for each kid to have one turn, then breaks in a snowfall of candy and confetti when one of the bigger kids takes a second turn. The older kids jump in to grab handfuls, and I shout, "There's enough for everyone, so leave some for the little kids!" before it disappears. The kids all scramble in together, laughing and jostling each other for candy, and I wonder what I know about their lives, really. What are they hiding? Are they all as happy as they look? Are there other people around keeping secrets like Ivan's?

I pick up a handful of candies and walk around to the front of the house to find Ivan and Jack and see if they are ready to send out the rafts.

The guys are already at the water, with the rafts piled high with wood. It's close to dark, so I say, "Are we ready?"

"I'll get everyone down," says Jack, and he walks up the beach to call the people to the water's edge.

"Do you have a wish?" I ask Ivan. We do this every year: light wooden rafts and send them out to sea. The idea is they burn out the old year and all the bad energy and sad things that have happened, and leave room for a new, better future.

Peter brought this tradition, or something like it, with him from Sweden, and we've adapted it to suit ourselves.

When everyone has gathered, we hand them slips of paper and pencils, and we each write a wish on our paper and tuck it between the logs on the pyres Jack and Ivan have built on top of the rafts. The tradition is that no one looks at each other's wishes, but I'm dying to know what Ivan has written, so I hand him my paper and say, "Swap?"

He grins and takes my paper. He smiles when he reads *My midsummer wish is for the sun and stars to smile down on me and Ivan.*

"Maddie, always so poetic."

"What is your wish?" I ask.

He folds over his paper and tries to hide it, but I grab it before he does and open it up. It says, *I wish life would get easier.*

Oh my.

"You weren't supposed to see that," he says.

There's nothing to say to that, so I run my hand across his beard and kiss his mouth as softly as I can, because my whole body aches to give him an easy world to live in, but a kiss is all I have to offer. Then I fold the paper back up again and add it to the wishes already tucked between the logs like dozens of white flags.

Jack steps forward and lights a bundle of sticks he's tied together. He uses that to light three others, then hands the torches to Ivan and Peter and Bo. "Ready?"

They nod, and the four of them push the rafts into the water, using the torches to light the pyres. A cheer goes up as the paper catches fire, and Bo and Peter push one raft and then the others out to sea.

It's not dark and not light. The horizon is a mirror, and we can't tell where sea ends and sky starts. We stand neither on land nor in water, but on something in between. This is the edge of the world. This is where magic lives, and if there is any place on earth where wishes are answered, this must be it.

We all stand together as the rafts burn into the night, fading slowly as they float away.

TWENTY-NINE

Ivan

I wake up when Willow pulls on my ear and says, "Wakey-wakey, sunshine."

"Shit, Jesus," I say before I realize it's her, but she doesn't seem to notice. She climbs up onto my bed and says, "Grandpa says I can spend the day with you."

"Oh" is all I can think of to say, though I know what I'm going to say to Pedro next time I see him.

"Where's Grandpa?" I ask.

"He went somewhere in the brown van with your daddy."

"So it's just the two of us. How long have you been here?"

"Since I got here," she says.

"What did you do when you got here?"

"Grandpa said I could watch TV, so I did, but then I got tired of that so I came to see if you were awake yet. You were snoring, so I knew you weren't."

I pull up the covers and move over so there's room for Willow next to me. She lies down with her head on my pillow and starts talking. I have no idea what she's saying, because in my head I'm cursing Pedro for leaving her with me. What was he thinking? Did he even check to see if I was here?

I reach out and search around for my phone.

"What time is it, sweetie?" I say, holding the phone out to Willow.

She takes it from me and turns it on, then says, "It's 11:00 AM. Time to get up and get going."

It's only been a few hours since I came back from the party. I struggle into a sitting position. "Where are we going?"

"To the playground. Then for ice cream, then to see the baby seals, then—"

"Wait, don't I get a say in what we do?"

"No," she says with a laugh.

"Can I at least eat before we go?"

"I'll make breakfast," she says, hopping off the bed.

I don't know what Willow thinks she can cook, so I swing my legs over the bed and get up too. Never mind that my head feels like a watermelon.

We go down to the kitchen, and I sit on a stool while Willow pours me a bowl of cereal and milk.

"That's a great breakfast, Willow," I say.

"I know."

She's so cute. She uses me like a climbing gym and pulls herself up until she's leaning right over the table.

"Watch out," I say, but she just grins and leans even farther. I guess, living with Pedro, she probably hasn't had anyone tell her not to do things.

"Are you done yet?" she asks after about two seconds.

"No," I say through a mouthful of cereal.

"Hurry up!"

"The playground isn't going anywhere, Willow."

She nods and pulls on my arm to speed me up.

* * *

By lunchtime I'm exhausted and starving, and Willow is super cranky, even though we did everything she asked to do.

"Let's head back to my place," I say, but she ignores me and keeps swinging.

"Come on, I'm hungry."

She keeps swinging.

"Do you want some more ice cream? Or some more candy?"

She keeps swinging, so finally I say, "Fine, well, I'm going anyway," and I turn and walk across the playground.

She's crying when she catches up with me, and I feel like a shit, even though I know I would have turned around if she hadn't followed me, so I say, "Maybe Grandpa will be back," and that seems to make her feel a bit better, because she stops sniveling.

We walk in silence back to my house, and I know before we get there that Pedro and Des are not back, because the van's not there.

"I guess they went on a long drive," I say.

"Maybe they're inside," she says.

"But there's no van."

"Maybe they left it somewhere and walked home."

"I guess," I say, even though I know it won't be true.

I let her lead me around the empty house, but when the tears start flowing again, I say, "Willow, you and me are going to go and find Maddie. Have you ever been to her house? She lives on the beach, and she has strawberries in her garden, and there's a telescope in the living room, and she's a painter."

I'm babbling, trying to find something that will make her stop crying, and the word *painter* seems to do it.

"Will she let me paint?" Willow asks.

"Yep, for sure."

She takes a big breath and pulls herself upright. "Okay," she says.

"You're an awesome kid," I say, because I can see how much effort she is making.

"I know."

We go as fast as we can down to the beach, then run together along the sand to Maddie's house. When we get to the deck, we both leap to the door and knock.

"Who's this?" asks Bo when he steps out onto the deck.

"That's Willow," I say.

"Hello, Willow," says Bo.

"Ivan said I can paint," Willow says, but Bo says, "Maddie's out for a few minutes, so you'll have to wait. How about you two come into the kitchen and join me for some lunch?"

"Thanks," I say. Without waiting for Willow to answer, I scoop her up and we follow Bo inside.

There's a small bookshelf in the kitchen filled with Maddie's old books, and Willow heads right for it.

"Do you want me to read you a book?" she says. When I nod, she chooses one with a turtle on the front and settles herself on a chair. She doesn't know how to read, so instead she makes up stories for each picture. Her soft voice is soothing and I try to listen, but soon my mind wanders and I start thinking about where Des and Pedro might be. Something must have happened. I mean, it's not like Des hasn't disappeared before, but for Pedro to leave Willow with me, that's something. Much as I hate to admit it, Pedro takes good care of Willow. She is Pedro's son's daughter, but I bet Pedro is a better grandfather than he was a father. He loves Willow. Thinking about this makes my heart race, because the more I think about it, the more I realize something really bad must have happened.

When Peter and Maddie arrive a few minutes later, I go off to the bathroom before we eat, and by the time I get back, Willow is telling them the story of how she got to ride in the bow of the boat on her way over here with her grandpa.

"I'm babysitting Willow for the day," I say.

But the looks on their faces tell me they know I'm lying.

THIRTY

Maddie

After lunch we take Willow into the living room, and as soon as she sees Bo's telescope, she wants to look through it. Peter and Bo help her adjust it to her eye, and she exclaims when the eagles on the headland pop into view. Watching them, I suddenly have a memory of when I was about the same age, and Bo brought this telescope home and I saw a falcon through the lens. I remember the magic of that, and the memory makes me smile.

Ivan and I leave the three of them and head out onto the deck.

"What's going on? How come you're looking after her?"

"She's visiting," he says, but there's absolutely no conviction in his voice.

Truly, Ivan is the most stubborn person I've ever met. The more questions I ask, the more silent he becomes, until he simply stares out to sea and doesn't say anything.

After a while, Willow comes outside and tugs on Ivan's arm and asks, "When is Grandpa coming?"

We exchange looks, but Ivan only shrugs, so I say, "Let's read a book, and maybe he'll be here when we're done."

She seems to think that's okay, because she hops up onto the railing and plays on it like it's a jungle gym.

In the end, Willow falls asleep on the window seat in the living room while I read to her, and Bo carries her to my bed, and we all agree that she should stay here for the night. Ivan leaves later on, but he still hasn't told me a damn thing about what's going on.

*   *   *

In the morning Willow wakes first, and though she tries to creep out of the bed, her movement wakes me.

"What time is it?" I ask her.

"Morning."

I yawn, but she hops around and says, "I have to pee," so I get out of bed and lead her to the bathroom.

Bo and Peter are still asleep. We all stayed up late last night, waiting for Pedro to show up, so I decide to let them be. When Willow is done in the bathroom, I say, "Let's go find Ivan, okay?"

"Is he at Grandpa's house?" Willow asks.

"No, he's at his house."

"I want to go home," Willow says.

I've seen Pedro and Willow around for, of course, and I know they live on one of the islands out across the channel, near Pitbull Island, but I don't know exactly where, so I say, "Let's go get Ivan, and he can help us."

Willow seems to see the sense in this, so she lets me lead her down the beach and then up the path to Ivan's house. The door is unlocked, and we go inside.

"Ivan," I call from the kitchen, but there's no answer, so Willow bellows out, "Ivan!" and the two of us giggle when there's a crashing sound upstairs.

"I'll go and get him," says Willow, but before I can stop her, she's running up the stairs. Following her is probably not the best idea, so instead I stay in the kitchen to see if there's anything to make for breakfast. It's a lot cleaner and tidier in here than it was the last time I came in, but still, it takes me a while to find a frying pan, and there's not much in the fridge except eggs. By the time Willow reappears with Ivan in tow, I've scrambled some eggs for us and made toast out of not-too-stale bread.

Ivan looks like he didn't get a lot of sleep last night.

"No sign of Pedro?" he asks.

I shake my head.

"He must be at home," Willow says. She climbs into a chair and pulls a plate full of eggs toward her. I guess she likes scrambled eggs. Ivan and I sit at the table with her and dig into our food. Willow talks nonstop while she's eating, chatting about the eagle's nest she and Pedro found in the forest. "I'll show you when I get home today," she says.

Ivan and I share a look that says, *Home today?*

"Willow, buddy, maybe you can stay with me another day or two," says Ivan. "I need help now that Des is away."

Willow eats another bite. "No, I want to go home today. Grandpa will be waiting for me."

"Ivan's daddy didn't come home last night. Maybe he's at your house," I say to Willow.

Ivan glares at me. "You think they're at Pedro's place?"

"I think we should go there and look," I say.

I can tell by the frown on Ivan's face that he is worried about that, but I think it's a good idea. Pedro's an old man. Maybe he's had an accident and is stuck out on his island, or maybe he and Des are there together, but for whatever reason they are not here, so something must have happened, and we should find out what. Willow seems to think so too, because she slides out of her chair and heads for the door.

"Wait," says Ivan. "I'll go and see if your grandpa is there. No need for you to come all the way out there."

Willow doesn't even slow down. She opens the door and walks out. Ivan follows her.

"Buddy, let me go. You don't want to go on a long boat ride, do you?"

"I want to go home."

"I think it would be better if I go first." Ivan tries to pick her up, but she holds her arms out straight and pushes him away. "I want to go home!" she wails.

Ivan looks at me for help, but I say, "She wants to go home, Ivan. Plus, you can't manage the boat alone."

"I can," he says.

"You can't," says Willow, which would be funny under other circumstances. Right now it makes Ivan grimace.

"Seriously, Maddie, I don't think it's a good idea. You and Willow should stay here and wait for Pedro and Des. I'll go and make sure there's nothing wrong out there."

"Ivan!" How can he say something like that in front of Willow? Willow whimpers and wipes tears from her eyes with the back of her hand, and I say, "We'll go find him, okay, Willow?"

"Okay, okay," says Ivan, but his eyes are dark, and I can tell he doesn't want us to go with him, so I say, "It's okay, Ivan. Whatever's going on, we're in it together now." Because apparently, sometime in the last few hours, I have decided that's true. Ivan snorts, but I say, "Truly, and besides, if Pedro isn't there, we should get some stuff for Willow, clothes and things."

"I could do that," he mumbles, but he reaches out and takes Willow's hand anyway.

"Let's go," says Willow.

* * *

Arne lets us take his boat. Ivan's driven it many times before and knows his way around it.

"I can drive it myself," he says as we clamber aboard.

"That's not the point, Ivan. You shouldn't have to be alone."

Willow and I sit up front. She's comfortable on the boat, which makes sense since she lives on an island, and she leans into the wind. I sit with my arm around her for safety and watch Ivan. He pays attention to the water, and once in a while he catches my eye. When he does, he smiles, but when he forgets I'm looking at him, he scowls. There's something out there he doesn't want us, or maybe just me, to see.

The island isn't far away, and before long Ivan noses the boat into a small dock. As soon as I lift Willow off the boat and help her unzip her life jacket, she runs up the dock, calling out, "Grandpa, I'm here." Ivan and I follow her as fast as we can, but we don't catch up to her until she's already inside.

"Grandpa!" she calls.

There's no answer.

"He might not be here, buddy," says Ivan.

Willow doesn't answer, just runs across the living room and through a door on the other side. Ivan follows her, but I stay in the living room, because it seems weird to be in someone's house uninvited.

It's funny how you form impressions of people and imagine how they live. Because Ivan dislikes Pedro so much, I thought his house would be dark or dirty or full of strange things, but it's clean and sunny and there's not a lot in the living room except for an expensive-looking sofa, a couple of matching chairs and a Persian rug. In one corner there's a bookshelf with some kids' books on it. I choose a small pile and put them on the sofa for Willow to look over. It seems obvious that she's going to have to come back to Bear Harbour with us, but convincing her to do so might be a problem, and I'm hoping the books will help.

When Ivan and Willow come back, Ivan's carrying Willow on one arm, and Willow is crying silently.

"He's not here?" I ask.

They both shake their heads.

"Good. That means you can come and have more sleepovers with me." I smile as broadly as I can without being totally fake, but Willow collapses onto Ivan's chest and puts her fingers in her mouth. Tears still stream down her face.

"I told her she could sleep in the big bed at my house," Ivan says.

"Well, even better then. And can I come?"

Willow nods, but she's clearly not too happy about this whole situation.

"There are lots of fun things we can do. We can feed Luseal at the wharf, and we can pick strawberries from my garden, and we can fix up that old swing on the beach..."

When I say the word *swing*, Willow lifts her head off Ivan's chest, so I say, "Willow, take me to your bedroom, and we'll pack some good clothes for swinging in."

Ivan lets her down, and she leads the way to the bedroom. She still isn't happy, but she's stopped crying. I turn around to ask Ivan if he can remember where we put the old swing, but he's already heading to another room. Looking for something he doesn't want to tell us about.

THIRTY-ONE

Ivan

We're in this together, Maddie says, but what if being in it together makes us part of a crime? Not that there's anything here. Pedro's house is strangely empty, but that doesn't mean there isn't anything to find. The weed Des and I took home last time I was here came from somewhere. Pedro must keep plants and some kind of harvesting machinery here. As soon as Willow and Maddie leave the room, I rush outside to the nearest shed but slow down before I open the door, because it occurs to me that if I'm going to see something gross or violent, it's going to be here. It takes a few deep breaths to psych myself up enough to open the door, and when I do, I take a deep breath and hold it. I've got no clue what I'm going to find in here, and I just hope to hell Pedro isn't in there bleeding to death. Or dead.

The door creaks open and I step inside slowly and flip the switch to turn on the light. I'm still holding my breath, but the room is empty. I mean completely. This shed looks like no one has been in here for years. This should make me happy, this total lack of weed or anything to do with it, but it doesn't, because I have no idea at all what that means. Was the shed always empty, or did Pedro clear it out?

I close the door behind me as I leave the shed, then walk around all the other outbuildings to see if there's nothing. This can't be good. No one around here has empty sheds. Most people's sheds are full of things like old furniture and bikes and gardening stuff—pots and bags of soil and shovels. Empty sheds. Who the hell's ever heard of that? It feels ominous, even more ominous than Pedro and Des leaving without telling us. Plus there's laundry from the line strewn around and caught in the salal bushes. I don't know what to make of this, but I decide not to say anything to Maddie when she and Willow come out to find me. Who knows what she might think.

"Did you find him?" asks Willow. Her face is stained with tears, she's pouty, and she's holding on to Maddie's hand.

On the spot, I decide to lie. "I found a letter. He must have forgotten to send it with you when you came to my house yesterday. He's gone away for a little while, and he'll be back soon. He says you get to come and stay with me while he's away."

Willow nods.

"And he says he wants us to have lots of fun."

"Did he say when he's coming back?" asks Maddie, which seems like a stupid thing to ask until I realize she thinks the letter is real.

"Soon," I say.

Maddie gives me a funny look but doesn't say any more about it. "We have clothes and toys for Willow. Do we need anything else?"

I've looked everywhere I can think of, and there's nothing here that tells us where they are, so I shake my head, and the three of us head back to the boat. Willow doesn't say anything for the whole trip back. It's not just that she's quiet—she's inside herself, like somewhere deep down she understands that she's in for more than a little vacation in Bear Harbour. I wonder if she remembers being abandoned the first time. It's so weird, though, because even though Pedro is totally flaky and mostly a person I hate, he's actually devoted to Willow. It makes me scared, because it seems like something big must have happened to make him go away like this.

When we get back to Bear Harbour, Maddie helps Willow gather her bags and lifts her off the boat. She holds out her hand for Willow to hold as they walk down the dock. I make sure the boat is closed and locked before I follow them.

"You should come have some lunch with us, Ivan," Maddie says as we walk along the boardwalk toward the beach to go home.

"Let's get Willow sorted out at my place first. Then we'll come join you for lunch."

"What do you mean, sorted out at your place?"

"I'll have to see if I can find some clean sheets for Des's bed for her to sleep in, and we might have to go grocery shopping for some breakfast foods." I don't bother telling her Des's room is a total mess. Willow won't care.

"We have the back room. She can sleep there," says Maddie.

"She can't stay at your place."

"Of course she can—why can't she?" Maddie says.

"I told her she could stay with me."

"It would be better for her to stay with me. There's food at my house. And clean sheets," she says.

Willow's head swivels back and forth between us as we speak, and now she says, "I'm going to stay with Ivan, so I can help now that Des is away, like you said."

Maddie doesn't say anything for a few steps, and then she says, "Fine."

I'm happy, because the less Peter and Bo see of Willow, the less they will wonder and the fewer questions they will ask. Who knows what kind of shit we're in for? The less they know, the better.

* * *

The day with Willow is fun. She's in a good mood after we make grilled cheese sandwiches for lunch, and Maddie and

I play with her for a while. After lunch Maddie says, "I think you should have a nap, Willow."

"I don't need to," says Willow, but Maddie says, "We'll read a story and see." She helps Willow choose a book from the pile they brought with them, and the two of them disappear upstairs to my bedroom. It's strange—after trying to keep people away from the house for years, now Maddie seems to be here all the time.

I only have time to check my phone for messages from Des or Pedro before Maddie comes back.

"She fell asleep before I finished the page," she says.

"I still haven't heard a thing."

Maddie frowns and gathers the plates from the table and takes them to the sink. She turns on the tap and pours soap into the water.

"You don't have to do that."

"I do." She picks up the first plate and scrubs at it, around and around, until it's way past clean, and I watch her do it, only slowly realizing that she's scrubbing to hide the fact that she's crying.

I come up behind her and gather her long hair into my hands and say, "Hey, Maddie, don't cry," but she shakes me off and says, "I'm not," through her tears.

"Why are you crying?"

"I'm not."

"You are." I lean over her and take the dishcloth from her hand, then turn her around until she's facing me. "Why are you crying?"

"Why do you think?"

That's not helpful, and it only makes things worse, because there are so many possible answers to that question. So many things seem wrong now, and the truth is, I don't want to think about any of them. Instead of answering, I wrap her hair around my wrist and stare at her feet. She unwraps my wrist, turns around and returns to the washing. There's just nothing to say, so I sit down and watch her.

When she's done, she says, "When Willow wakes up we should get out of your house, get some air."

"You don't have to stay," I say, but I know it's the wrong thing to say as soon as the words are spoken, so I shake my head. "No, I don't mean that," and she looks at me funny and the two of us just stare at each other because neither of us knows what is going on or how the hell to cope with it or what to do or how to get out of it. And just as I'm thinking I should tell her that she doesn't have to make this problem hers, she shakes her head, takes a deep breath and says, "Never say that."

"Say what?"

"That it's not my problem."

"Shit, Maddie, how do you always know what I'm thinking?"

"It's written all over your face, Ivan. So promise me. We're in this together, right?" She takes my hand as she speaks and stares right into my eyes, so the only thing I can do is smile at her and say, "Right."

If having someone help me could make all this go away, she'd be the person to help for sure.

When Willow wakes up she opts for the playground, and the three of us head out. I haven't spent this much time at the playground since I was about six years old. She runs straight to the swings and hops on. Maddie sits on the other swing, and the two of them pump themselves as high as they can go. I sit on the merry-go-round and watch their hair streaming behind them. Willow squeals and Maddie laughs, and for the seconds that they are flying, I'm happy. Then, as always happens, every single time, reality returns, this time when Willow falls and scrapes her arm.

She wails, and I can see a long day of screaming ahead. So I say, "Willow, how about some ice cream?"

"Yes!" Willow's mood shifts immediately, and she picks herself up and rubs the sand off her arm, and we head to the ice-cream store for the millionth time.

* * *

After three days, Willow is driving me crazy. She tries to help, and she's pretty independent, but most of her help makes things worse, and then I have to fix whatever she's messed up, but she's always standing right where I want to be, and I keep almost tripping over her. At breakfast I burn the eggs because she's in the way and I can't get the pan off the burner fast enough. Willow pushes the eggs around on her plate but won't eat them.

"That's not how Grandpa makes eggs," she says.

"I know. I burned them."

"I'll make some cereal," she says.

I pull down two bowls and let her at it. Why not have cereal? There aren't any eggs left. As I eat, I contemplate what we are going to do today. What do little girls like to do with their days other than go to the playground? I can't handle the playground again. What did she say she wanted to do the first morning she was here? Only three days ago, though it seems like ages.

Willow doesn't eat her cereal either. She dips her spoon into it but dunks it back into the milk rather than eating it.

"When's Grandpa coming back?" she asks for the millionth time. I grit my teeth, because I have no answer.

"Want to go to the playground?" I ask.

She smiles, which is good, because I'm not up for a day of moping. "I'll get my shoes," she says.

"Can you bring me mine too?" I ask as I swallow a few spoonfuls of cereal.

Willow helps me tie my shoes and does a pretty good job of her own, and we head out of the house. We take the road instead of the beach, because it's quicker, and Willow is enthusiastic about getting to the playground. There are a bunch of kids already there, and Willow seems to know some of them, so she skips off to play, and I sit on a bench to watch.

Willow's holding it together pretty well, but the truth is, I'm not. I haven't slept in three days, and the only thing I've eaten is cereal. Maddie comes by several times a day and plays with Willow, which is helpful, but it leaves me more time to contemplate what's happened to Des and Pedro. Des has disappeared before, but not for more than a night without some kind of message. I've texted a million times and tried to call, but he hasn't answered.

When it starts to rain, I say to Willow, "Okay, buddy, time to go back to my house."

She ignores me and continues to swing.

"Willow!"

She keeps pumping her legs in the air.

That's it. I can't take it anymore.

"Willow, buddy," I call. "Let's go to the library."

"I don't want to," she says.

"Too bad. We're going." At this point I'd grab her swing and make her get off, even though there's a bunch of moms standing around who would probably shout at me, but Willow seems to sense I mean it, so she hops off the swing and follows me across the park to the library. I guess Pedro's taken her there before, because she heads right for the little corner where the kids' books are and finds herself a cushion to sit on. There's a story time going on, so I ask the lady behind the desk if I can leave Willow there for a bit.

"Story time is half an hour. Be back by then."

It only takes me a few minutes to get home, and a couple more to rush up the stairs, pull the backpack out from under my bed and check to make sure it has a hoodie and a toothbrush. There's a small stash of money in my wallet. It takes me another few minutes to get out onto the road, but then it takes another fifteen minutes for a car to come by. It's a white Chevy that I recognize as Noah's mom's. It's visible for about two minutes before it reaches me, and in that time I change my mind four times. When she does finally approach me, she slows and rolls down her window.

"Need a lift to Port Alberni?"

I could run away so easily. Ride to Port Alberni, catch a bus to Nanaimo and a ferry to Vancouver and disappear. It would be so easy. But then I'd be just like my mother, abandoning a kid who needs me. Just like Des, incapable of seeing things through.

"Ivan?"

My palms are sweaty, and I can feel my heart pounding. It would be so easy. "No, thanks, just out for a walk," I say.

"Need anything at Costco?"

"Crunchy peanut butter, if you come across some."

She adds that to a paper list she has on the passenger seat and says, "You can pick it up tonight." She smiles and drives on.

I hike the strap of my pack to make it tighter and turn back to town.

I'm five minutes late for Willow. The lady behind the counter glares at me, but Willow doesn't seem to have noticed that I'm late. She's on a cushion by the window, looking at a book. I sit down next to her. "How was story time?"

"We read a story about a crab who doesn't want to grow into his new shell."

I have no idea what she's talking about. "Did you like it?"

"Yes, and this one's about a bear who gets left behind at the bus stop because no one wants him. He's like you and me," she says.

Oh, shit, shit, shit. How can she know that? I pick her up and put her on my lap. Her hair smells like baby shampoo. "Good thing we have each other then," I say, because it's true.

"And Maddie," she says.

"And Maddie."

Willow stands up and straightens her leggings, then sits back down on my lap. "Can you read it to me, please?"

I open the book and start at page one.

THIRTY-TWO

Maddie

It breaks my heart seeing Ivan so lost. He wanders around aimlessly with his little sidekick Willow, the two of them just pacing through time. At first, even though it was worrisome that Des and Pedro were gone, there was an edge of fun to having Willow, something like playing house. Somehow, all three of us seemed to be able to push away the fear and worry and just pretend, but not anymore. Noah's mom told me she saw Ivan walking on the highway and he looked like he was heading out of town, but when she offered him a lift he said he was just out for a walk. Even though I don't like to admit it, I think he was running away. He and Willow have been inseparable since then, and he won't talk about what happened to make him come back. I haven't had a chance to talk to Ivan in private for three days, and when I try to talk to him, he changes the subject, though I doubt Willow has any real understanding of what's going on anyway. How could she? She's only five.

I can't even imagine what the two of them are going through.

"Hello, Maddie," says Willow when she opens the door this morning. She's wearing the same clothes she was wearing yesterday, though I brought a bunch with us from the island.

"Hi, Willow, how's it hanging?" She likes clichés, and I love the way she answers them.

"It's hanging low." She points to Ivan, who's half asleep on the sofa.

"Bad night?"

"He didn't sleep much."

Ivan looks up as I enter the room. He is obviously exhausted; the skin is purple below his eyes, and his face is puffy. He smiles at me but doesn't sit up.

"Willow, buddy, why don't you come and stay at my house for a while?" I say.

"It's okay," Ivan says.

"She'll be fine."

"No," he says, and this time he does sit up.

"I'm not trying to steal her," I say.

Ivan leans back in the sofa and says, "Sorry, I know."

"What's going on, Ivan? Has something happened?"

He shakes his head, but he's lying. I'm sure of it.

"Willow, honey, how about you go choose some clean clothes so I can wash those ones?" I say.

"Do I have to?"

"Yes, please, your clothes are upstairs. You know where they are."

She nods and runs up the stairs, and I sit beside Ivan and say, "Okay, she's out of the room. Now tell me."

"Nothing happened, Maddie."

I study his face, trying to decipher what's there, but he won't look at me properly, so I say, "We have to tell someone."

"No."

"Ivan, we have to."

"No way."

"You have no idea what's happened or how long they'll be gone. We have to, otherwise it's like we've kidnapped her or something."

"Des is on his way back. I'll talk to him when he gets here."

"You're lying."

He doesn't respond. But enough is enough. He looks so beaten, and he shouldn't be shouldering this. It's not fair to him or to Willow. "You tell someone or I will," I say. He turns away from me and puts his arms over his head.

When Willow comes downstairs, I take her over to my house, where Bo and Peter are delighted to see her, as I knew they would be. The four of us spend a couple of hours looking through the telescope and searching for shells on the beach and counting crabs. After lunch, Willow goes to sleep in my bed, and I head back to Ivan's place.

The door's not locked, so I walk in. Ivan's still asleep on the sofa. He looks peaceful, for once, so I leave him be. Probably sleep is the best thing for him.

Ivan sleeps for the whole day, and in the evening when I go back for a third time to check on him, he's awake and demands Willow back.

"She's with Kyra and Laurie. They're babysitting for the night, and you're spending the evening with me," I say.

Ivan shakes his head and says, "I'd better go get her. I don't want her to think I've abandoned her or something." He goes into the front hallway and pulls on his shoes.

"She was happy to spend the night with the girls, Ivan."

I follow him out of the house and down the driveway to the road.

"Yeah. Well..."

"You feel responsible for her, don't you?" I ask.

"How could I not? Don't you?"

I don't want Ivan to go and get Willow. I want him to relax, to spend the evening with me or Jack or Noah. To enjoy himself for once. I hate to see him like this. It tears at my heart.

"Ivan, I meant what I said earlier. I'm starting to get worried about Des and Pedro. I mean, something must have happened, right, to keep them away this long? Has Pedro ever done anything like this before? We should tell someone."

"No," he says and keeps walking.

Argh…he makes me want to tear my hair out. "What about Willow, Ivan?"

"What about her?"

"She misses her grandfather."

"I know," he says, but his face turns a little gray when he says it, like it's the first time he's thought of that.

"Why are you being like this, Ivan?"

Ivan stops and runs his hands over his eyes. "Do you know what she said to me in the library yesterday? I came back to pick her up after the story time, and she held up a book about Paddington Bear and said he was left behind because no one wanted him, just like her and me."

My heart skips a beat when he says that. Oh my god, imagine a little kid saying something like that. And the look on Ivan's face. Devastated.

"Do you think it's true?"

"Don't you?"

What on earth can I say to that? How do I say, *Yes, in fact, I think your dad and Willow's grandfather have run away?*

"Have you heard from Des?" I ask instead.

He shakes his head.

"So you think they're together?"

"You think they might not be?"

"I don't know what to think."

"Me either."

He runs his hands through his hair and starts walking again. I walk beside him, saying nothing. There's nothing to say.

* * *

When we get to Noah's house, Willow's having so much fun that I'm able to convince Ivan she won't feel abandoned just because she's spending the night with the girls. For the first time in days, he seems happy.

We head to Jack's house. "Ivan, haven't seen you in ages," says Jack as we walk into the kitchen. Ivan shrugs but doesn't explain, so neither do I.

"Hungry?" says Jack. They've obviously just finished dinner. I've eaten, but Ivan hasn't, so we both sit down at the table. Arne pours me a glass of wine, which makes me laugh, because he knows how old I am, and Jack spoons a bunch of food onto a plate for Ivan.

"What have you two been up to?" Arne asks.

Without a pause, Ivan says, "Pedro's granddaughter has been staying with me for a bit. Pedro and Des had to go away on some business, so he asked if I'd keep her for a while. She's cute but tiring. Maddie's helping out too."

The story slips so quickly out of his mouth, it makes me shudder. What kind of life makes him lie so easily? Ivan looks at me to corroborate his story, so I smile and nod, like I'm agreeing with everything he says. I don't lie as easily as that, so I close my mouth and look at my glass. I don't want anyone seeing the look on my face.

THIRTY-THREE

Ivan

Maddie's mad at me, I know, because last night I drank as much as my body could hold and then some. I drank until all this fucking shit disappeared, and the only things that mattered were the shapes of the stars in the sky. I don't remember anything else, not even how I got home. The only thing I do remember is waking up in the middle of the night with a shit-awful hangover and drinking glasses of water, then staggering back to bed.

Today after Kyra brought Willow back, she and I had a quiet day. Mostly we watched movies on Netflix. I told her I'm sick, so she read to me and pretty much left me alone. In the evening she fell asleep on the sofa, and now I've tucked her into Des's bed for the night. She's so little I can hardly even tell there's a person in there. I should go to my own bed, but instead I lie next to Willow and watch her breathe. The thought that runs through my head all night as I drift in and out of sleep has nothing to do with having Willow here or arguing with Maddie. It's about how peaceful it is when Des isn't around.

* * *

In the morning I find Des sitting at the kitchen table eating cereal.

"There's no more milk," he says. I pull out a chair and sit across the table from him. I have no idea—none at all—what to say.

"Aren't you going to say hello?" Des asks.

I shake my head. "I don't even know where to start."

"Welcome back is a good place."

"When did you get back?"

"Ten minutes ago," he says, though the plates and bowls say otherwise.

A million thoughts run through my head, everything from grabbing my bag and running to hoping it's all over now, but the words that come out of my mouth are "Willow's asleep in your bed," because that about sums it up.

"Yeah, I'm sorry about that. Leaving her here, I mean. It seemed the safest thing to do. We knew you'd take good care of her."

"Fuck, Des!" I leap out of my chair and throw a plate across the room. It crashes against the kitchen wall. "Did you even check to make sure I was home that day?"

He frowns. "I'm sure we did."

"Why'd you come home now? Where's Pedro?"

The silence lasts so long I figure he's not going to answer, but then he says, "I thought I'd better come back. Make things right."

Like that's going to make anything better.

"How are you planning to do that?" My hands are clenched so tight my knuckles ache.

He stares at the table as he says, "I don't know. I screwed up, Ivan. Big-time. But I've learned my lesson this time. I know I haven't been a good father to you, not for a long time. I know. And being away gave me time to think about that, and that's why I came back. For you. To put things right or at least to try."

Well, holy shit. I can't even respond to that. Instead, I pick up the chair that toppled when I leaped out of it and place it upright. Then I take a deep breath to steady myself and leave the room.

* * *

When I come back inside an hour later, Willow and Des are chatting each other up in the kitchen. He's tying her shoelaces, and as I walk in he says, "I'm taking Willow out for breakfast, then over to Peter and Bo's. Thought you could use a break."

"Your daddy says I can have pancakes!" Willow says.

"Does he?" I eye Des. Why is he doing this? I'm not sure if it's okay to leave Willow with Des, but then, I've survived being with him, and as she jumps up and down in excitement, I simply say, "Okay."

Des smiles at me as he follows Willow out the door. So maybe he is trying.

* * *

There's a whole pile of things I'm supposed to be making for people, but when I walk around the house to the back, where the wood and tools are ready and waiting for me, I don't know where to start. I'm so shit tired and worn out that I can't even think about it. The only thing I can do is go back inside, sink into the sofa and close my eyes.

Later I get up and walk over to Arne's house, where I ask for the key to his boat. It doesn't take long to get over to Pedro's dock, cinch the rope and head to his place. The grass is tall and brown now, and the laundry's blown off the line and all across the yard. I can tell from a glance that no one has been here.

I don't care about the house; I want to take a look at the sheds again, so I cross the yard and pull open the door to the closest one. I don't know what I thought I would see, but there's nothing. Totally nothing. The next one is empty too, and the next. They're just empty, all of them. Same as before. Everything in the house looks just like it did when Maddie and Willow and I were here before.

What did I think I'd find?

Answers?

I take the ride back to town slowly. It's a sunny day, the kind my mom used to like to go for boat rides on. We'd gang up on Des and beg him to take us out, and then Mom would pack a picnic, and the three of us would head over to an island and hang out for the day. There were always seagulls. And crab shells on the shore, and bits of sea glass that I'd gather and give to her. These are the stupid things I remember, like it was some golden time, but it must not always have been like that, because otherwise she wouldn't have left.

I don't know why I'm thinking about my mom now, except that maybe for the first time ever I kind of understand her. Maybe she left because she felt like I'm feeling now. Like there's no way out of this. Like any choice I make is going to be the wrong one. Like why did this problem have to become mine?

And who the fuck does Des think he is, abandoning me and then coming back like this? I've been taking care of Des for years, since long before I was really able to. I've come home every night of my life to check and make sure he hasn't fallen down the stairs or choked on his own vomit or burned the house down. And yet every day he's gone into town and made people believe everything was okay. Sure, they know he drinks. Everyone knows that, and everyone's a little bit upset about it. A little bit. Not enough to check it out. Not enough to stop it. I've never understood how so many people can see but not understand.

And now Des is back from whatever he was doing with Pedro, looking sorry. But shit, I've seen that look so many times, I know better than to trust it. If only my mind could tell my heart that.

And as for my mom, she could have taken me with her.

THIRTY-FOUR

Maddie

I know before Ivan makes it to the top of the stairs onto the deck that something is wrong. It's in his face, in the way he moves. The slow drag of his step.

"I went to the island to look for Pedro," he says.

Willow runs up to him and tugs on his shirt, and when he looks down at her and shakes his head, it's like something falls out of her. I would have expected crying and screaming. Instead, she goes limp, and Ivan has to catch her as she falls.

"He'll come back soon, sweetie, I just know it," he says as he scoops her up, but I wonder, as I listen to his words, if he believes what he's saying. The two of them, they're so hopeful it tears my heart in pieces to see it. Ivan sits down on one of the deck chairs with Willow on his lap.

"I'm thinking ice cream," he says, but Willow doesn't respond. It's like she's gone inside herself, and that's way, way more scary than if she cried.

"How about the playground?" I say, but she doesn't even look at me.

"Do you want to look through the telescope?" Ivan asks.

"Or we could make a cake."

Willow doesn't respond to any of our suggestions, and in the end we sit together in silence and listen to the waves slash at the shore.

* * *

Bo and Peter come back later to find Ivan and Willow asleep in their chair and me sketching them. Bo traces his finger along the pencil line of Ivan's arm curling around Willow and smiles.

Peter passes me a bag of groceries and says, "What happened to them?" as I follow him into the kitchen.

"Willow thought Pedro was coming home today, but he's not here yet. She was upset."

"He's been gone quite a long time," Peter says.

"Yeah, it's been a while." It's hard to keep the frustration out of my voice.

"It's not fair to expect Ivan to keep looking after her for so long. When is Pedro coming back?" Peter asks.

"Oh, soon, I expect," I say. I hate the lying. I hate how easily I do it. I open my mouth to tell him everything, then close it again.

"I hope so," says Peter. He folds the grocery bag and heads back out for the next one.

When he returns, Peter hands me an envelope from Emily Carr University.

With all the stuff going on with Willow and Ivan, I haven't been thinking straight, and I don't know what to say when I take the package. Will I still go to Emily Carr if I can't convince Ivan to come to Vancouver with me? Should I go and make Peter and Bo happy or stay with Ivan? Would it make any difference to him? And what about travelling around and seeing the Louvre and all those other museums?

"I'll look at it later," I tell Peter. I can't think about university right now.

* * *

We make a convoy across the beach. We've had some lunch, but we're all still worn out from Willow's disappointment, so we walk in silence, and by the time we reach Ivan's house, Willow has fallen asleep again on Ivan's back. We head into the house and tuck Willow into Ivan's bed. She's so little. Both Ivan and I stare at her sleeping, and I know we're both wishing we could protect her from all of this.

Des is out back. He chokes the saw and pulls the safety glasses off his face when we come around the corner.

"Hey," says Ivan. The air is thick between them, and no wonder. I reach for Ivan's hand and squeeze it.

"You're behind on these," Des says.

Ivan's face turns red, and he tightens his fist around my fingers, but he takes a deep breath and says, "I was busy."

Des ignores that comment and says, "I thought I'd spend the day working here, catch you up a bit. Did Jack text you? He says he's heading over to Riley Point later. You two should go."

Emotions rush across Ivan's face so fast I can't follow them, but when they stop he says, "Willow will wake up in half an hour or so."

"Okay, I'll work until then," says Des.

Ivan isn't convinced, but a break is what he needs, so I say, "Let's get our stuff."

He glances at me as if to say, *Do you think so?*

So I smile, and he relents.

* * *

The surf is great. At Riley Point the waves break in straight lines and the sets come in evenly, and there's always a bit of a rip tide on the east side of the point that we use to paddle out to the green. There are five of us today: Jack, Noah, Bea, myself and Ivan, and we all sit on our boards and watch the sun sparkle on the water as we wait for the next set. Jack and Noah and Bea catch waves when they come, but Ivan and I just sit there like we're both too tired to surf. And I guess we are.

"Ivan," I say.

"Hmm…"

"Remember that day you put stones along my arms and legs?"

"Yeah?"

"Nothing. Just remembering."

Ivan sits up and paddles his board up next to mine. He leans over and gives me a big smooch on my cheek. It makes me laugh.

*   *   *

When the sun is low, Ivan and I surf in to shore and join the others on the beach. Jack and Bea are already changed, and Jack says, "I have to get back," so Ivan and Noah and I get out of our wet suits and into our clothes, and we all head back into town.

"I'll get off here," I say when Jack pulls up at Ivan's house. We store the boards behind the house and hang the wet suits across the banisters of the back stairs to dry.

"Looks like he got a lot done," I say to Ivan. A half-built cabinet sits under the tree.

"We were gone most of the day," Ivan says.

"Well, it's good, isn't it? That he did this?"

"Yeah." Ivan runs his hands along the wood.

It looks beautiful to me.

"He's so good at it," I say.

"Yeah."

"Doesn't he have his own job, though?"

"He did."

Ivan doesn't elaborate, so I say, "But?"

"His record at keeping jobs isn't good."

I didn't know that. I've always thought Des takes seasonal work so he'll have time to do carpentry, but maybe that's not so. Now's not the time to ask, though. We've been back in Bear Harbour for five minutes, and already reality is pushing back on Ivan, and his body has lost its easy surfing feel.

"I'll go check on Willow," he says. Ah, so that's it.

We walk back around the house to the front door and go inside.

"Des! Willow!" Ivan calls out, but there's no answer.

"Maybe they're upstairs, or they've gone out," I say, but Ivan's already tearing through the house, ripping open doors. When he rushes past me and charges up the stairs, I follow him, and there's Willow, the tiniest puddle of a person, huddled in the doorway to Ivan's bedroom, sobbing and gulping.

"Willow!" Ivan scoops her up and hugs her to his chest, and I throw my arms around them so we're all crushed together. Willow wails so loudly the sound blocks out everything else in the world, and her little heart beats fast, like a bird's.

"I'll fucking kill him," Ivan says.

"Honey, how long have you been alone?" I ask, but she wails again and again, letting out all that anger and fear in one sound. Her pants are wet, and there's snot across her face. She's been alone for a while, and she won't forget this, just as I can see from how hard Ivan's shaking that he's been here before, and he has not forgotten.

It takes my breath away, and my own sobs come out jagged and rough.

"I'll fucking kill him," he says again.

I'll help.

THIRTY-FIVE

Ivan

Seeing Willow huddled in the doorway of my room makes me snap. I hold her so tightly I can't breathe, and she's heavy like lead in my arms.

"I'll fucking kill him," I say.

Maddie gets this look in her eyes like she'll beat me to it, and Willow sobs even louder. I start shaking, first in my arms, then my legs, then my whole body, and Maddie shifts so she's carrying Willow's weight and says, "Go, Ivan," and I shove Willow into Maddie's arms and head down the stairs and out of the house and down to the beach, where I can breathe. The tide is low, and I run hard and fast into the driftwood and onto the path at the end of the beach, past Maddie's house, over roots and twigs, until the path peters out and I'm running through salal and sword ferns. Their resistance is a relief, so I push and pull at them as I go deeper into the forest, and I feel like I can run away forever, through the forest and all the way to Victoria. I want to run until I don't know anything anymore and am nowhere and no one knows me. I want to run until I disappear.

I run on. My shoes and jeans are soaked. I'm crashing now over stumps and downed logs and around trees surrounded by sharp ferns, and I don't have any breath at all anymore, so I'm lurching instead of running, but at last I run out of the forest and stumble onto the highway. The woods continue on the other side, but when I come out of the trees, something inside me stops, and I have to sit and cry.

I cry until I'm dry inside. Until there's no point anymore. Then I look to the highway leading to Port Alberni, to Victoria and beyond. If a car comes, I'll take it.

No I won't. Running away. That's the one thing I could never forgive myself for doing.

* * *

Neither Willow nor Maddie says anything when I come in. They're watching something on the TV. There's no sign of Des. I'm shaking with cold, so I take a shower and change before I join them in the living room.

When I come back, Maddie leaves Willow in the living room and we go into the kitchen.

"Any sign of Des?" I ask.

She shakes her head.

"Now will you tell someone?" she asks.

But she doesn't get it. No one does. No one ever has.

I shake my head.

She gasps and looks away. "Oh, Ivan."

"You think that just because Des is a jerk I don't love him? That I can abandon him? I'll kill him for sure. But I can't walk away."

"No, I…no, that's not what I mean," says Maddie.

"You and Bo and Peter, what you have is special, Maddie. You all believe in each other. Don't you think Des deserves someone in the world who believes in him too? My mom didn't, obviously. No one else around here does. Even he doesn't. He can't keep a job or remember he's supposed to be taking care of a kid. He's a fucking disaster. Of course no one believes in him, but someone has to."

Maddie's voice is tiny when she picks up my shaking hand and says, "But Ivan, why does it have to be you?"

"Because it's always been me," I say.

"But why?"

"Because he's all I've got."

THIRTY-SIX

Maddie

This is what emptiness feels like. No way forward, no way back. Nothing I can do to make it better. Nothing I can do to make it go away. I finally understand what we've all abandoned Ivan to. How we've betrayed him for so many years. How blind we've all been.

"You can't go on like this, Ivan, you can't."

He doesn't answer me.

"You're not alone, Ivan."

"But I am."

"It's not okay what he did, leaving Willow like that. She was terrified."

"I agree. When I see him I'll kill him," Ivan says.

"So you agree that what he did to Willow is wrong, not okay."

"Of course I agree."

"But Ivan, if it's not okay for him to do that to her, it's also not okay for him to do it to you."

My words hit him like sand in the eye, and he flinches.

"You better go," he says.

And I don't understand.

* * *

It's late when I get home, but both Bo and Peter are on the deck, so I can't avoid them.

"What happened? Are you okay?" Peter asks, because I guess I'm wearing the fact that I'm totally not okay all over my face. "We saw Ivan running past a while ago. He looked terrified."

Bo puts down his mug and stands up, blocking my way back down the stairs. "Tell us now, Maddie. Enough is enough," he says.

So this is it.

My hands shake as I say, "Des and Pedro disappeared almost a week ago. Ivan had no idea where they were or when they were coming back. He didn't even know that they were going or that Willow was going to be staying with him. Des came home this morning to say he was sorry and he wanted to make amends, but when we took Willow back there for her nap this afternoon and left her with him, he took off and left her alone. We found her when we got back from surfing. She was terrified. Ivan was so upset."

That hardly explains it, but it's the best I can do.

Peter takes a deep breath. Bo puts his arm across Peter's shoulders, and I'm not sure if he's comforting Peter or steadying himself.

"Des wouldn't do that," Peter says, but I shake my head. "He did."

"But…"

"We've known Des a long time, Maddie. Since you and Ivan were tiny children. He's had his struggles, we know, but this…" Bo's voice is heavy, and his brow is creased.

"We see him almost every day," Peter says.

"And miss everything," I say.

Peter gasps. "That's not fair," he says.

"Well, it's true, isn't it?"

"What exactly have we missed?" Bo says.

"That Des is an alcoholic and can't take care of himself or Ivan."

"I mean, we know he drinks. We've talked to him about it," Peter says. "We thought he had it under control."

"Ivan hid it for him," I say. "He hid how bad it was." The truth of my words hits them, because both of them sag, and Bo sits down, and I can't help saying, "You should have known."

THIRTY-SEVEN

Ivan

Willow and I make it through the night, and in the morning we have cereal like always.

"Do you want to go to the playground today, Willow?" I ask. I'm so tired I'm shaky, but I'm not letting her out of my sight again. She starts to answer me, but then someone knocks at the door, so she hops right off her chair and runs toward the door.

"Wait." I scoop her up as she passes.

I hoist her onto my hip and go to the door. For some reason, don't ask me why, I decide to look out the peephole before I answer the door. It's Pedro, with Des coming up behind him. I don't think the word *anger* covers what I'm feeling right now.

"Hold on, buddy," I say. I take a deep breath and open the door.

"Hey there, Willow," Pedro says. Des moves to walk in the door, and Willow stiffens in my arms so that it's hard to hold on to her.

"Let's go home, eh?" Pedro says.

But Willow burrows into my chest. She's got a death grip on my neck, making it hard for me to breathe.

"I brought you some candy," Pedro says.

Neither Des nor I say anything, but I kick the door and shut it on them.

"Hey!" I hear Des shout from outside.

"Let's go out the back way," I say to Willow. "We'll run down the garden and straight to the playground."

Willow doesn't say anything, and she's still got her death grip on me, so I make my way to the back. As soon as we get outside, Des and Pedro come around the side of the house, so I hitch Willow around to my back and run.

"I'll call the police," Pedro says, which is a bunch of bullshit, but still, I run faster.

"Come on, Willow," Des says. Pedro and Des are coming up fast behind us, and it's hard to run with Willow bouncing on my back. She's still clutching me so tightly I'm having trouble breathing, and her heart is beating so fast it feels like it's going to explode.

Des is fast, and he's catching up with us, so I veer to the right and duck into the forest. There's no point in sticking to the trails—Des knows them as well as I do—so I scramble over a fallen tree and head downhill. Des keeps calling after us, but his voice grows fainter as he loses track of us.

I slow down and pick my way through the undergrowth. My lungs ache for air. I stop and bend down so Willow can get off my back, but she just hangs there, frozen in position, arms wrapped around my neck.

"Ivan!" Des's voice is closer than I'd like, so I shift Willow back into position and keep moving. The undergrowth is thicker here, and the slope gets steeper the closer we get to the beach. I need both hands to grab onto roots and branches. My foot slips, and suddenly we're falling. Willow screams, and I land badly in the roots of a fallen tree, my whole weight on my arm. I swear I can hear it crack. Pain bursts through me, so I hardly remember to roll away from Willow. She's still screaming, and I don't want Des to hear her, so I grab her arm and shout, "Shut up, Willow."

Her eyes go wide and she gulps huge sobs, but she does stop screaming. I'm tangled in roots and ferns, and my arm feels like it's got a sword sticking through it. It's hard not to scream and gulp and sob like Willow, and all I can do is lie back and wait for the pain to subside.

"I'm so sorry, I'm so sorry," I say over and over once I can speak again. There's no sound of Des, and I hope he and Pedro have gone away.

She doesn't say anything.

"I think I broke my arm," I say.

She just looks at me, her eyes still wide.

"Let's find Maddie," I say, because that's the only thing I can think of.

Willow nods and tries to climb onto me again, but I can't carry her with my arm broken, so instead she helps me up and we stumble the rest of the way through the forest until we reach the beach, then run together to Maddie's house.

My arm is killing me, and I'm finding it hard to think, so when we get there I let her knock on the door, and I sit on the edge of the deck and wait for someone to come.

"What's this?" asks Bo when he steps out onto the deck.

"Ivan broke his arm," says Willow.

"What? Let's take a look," says Bo, and he strides over to where I've collapsed and peers at my arm, which is pretty swollen.

"This is going to need X-rays. What on earth were you doing?"

"We were running away," says Willow, which I would not have told Bo.

"What!"

"It was super scary," she says.

"What on earth?" says Bo.

"Can you please go get Maddie?" I say.

"She's in town with Bea," he says, and it's the last straw. I start to cry, even though I haven't cried in public since I was about six.

"Where's Des?" asks Bo.

"He's probably up at the house. Maybe. I don't know."

"Let's get you to the clinic," says Bo, and he takes my elbow and helps me stand. He and Willow and I walk up the road and get into the car, and he drives us to the clinic in town.

"Willow, you keep Ivan company, okay? I'm going to find Maddie," says Bo after we've checked in and are sitting in the waiting room. Willow nods her head solemnly and sits next to me.

"Do you want me to read you a book?" she asks. When I nod, she chooses *Winnie-the-Pooh* from a pile of books and pulls it onto her lap.

When Bo arrives with Maddie, she sits down next to me and takes my hand. "I hear you think you're Superman." She's trying to make me laugh, but the best I can do is smile at her and squeeze her hand.

"Does it hurt a lot?" she asks.

"Like a son of a bitch."

"I'll see if I can get you something for the pain," says Bo. He puts out his hand for Willow, who hops up and takes it, and the two of them go in search of a nurse.

"What on earth were you doing?" Maddie asks.

"Trying to escape."

"From what?"

"From who, you should ask." I want to tell Maddie the whole story, but my mind is too focused on the pain in my arm, so instead I put my head in her lap and close my eyes. She runs her hand through my hair and doesn't say anything.

THIRTY-EIGHT

Maddie

Ivan's swept away by painkillers. He moves in slow motion, and his voice is thick, and I'm not sure if it's because he's drugged or because of what's happened that he collapses into a deep sleep even while he's waiting for the cast. He rouses a bit when the doctor comes in and sets the arm and puts on the plaster, but I'm not sure he knows what's going on. I am sure he doesn't know Des is there, watching everything, or that Pedro's come too.

When Des leaves the room to go to the bathroom, Pedro sits down next to me and says, "Hi, Willow. I brought you some candy."

She stays on my lap but accepts the candy.

"I'm sorry you were scared earlier when we came to the house. I should have told you I was coming. Silly Grandpa, eh?"

Willow nods and sticks a piece of candy in her mouth. Bo, Peter and I all watch, and though I am silent, my heart is racing. I have a million things to say, but I don't want to scare Willow any more than she's already been scared today.

"You didn't get hurt when you ran away, did you?" Pedro asks. Willow shakes her head.

"Were you trying to fly? How high did you get before you fell? I flew once, but I didn't get very far," Pedro says.

"People can't fly," Willow says.

"No? Oh, I wonder what it was that I did then. It sure felt like flying."

Willow laughs, and I see this is how it's going to be. When Willow tries to stand up to follow Pedro out, I clutch her and hold her tightly to me. Bo stands, and so does Peter, but Pedro bends down so he's looking at me face-to-face and says, "She's my granddaughter, and I have legal custody of her."

"She enjoyed staying with the kids, Pedro. Maybe she should stay for a while, just until you get yourself sorted out," Bo says.

Pedro reaches out his hand to Willow, who slips off my lap and takes it.

"See you later, alligator," Willow says.

"In a while, crocodile," I reply, and they walk out the door.

We all stand in silence as they make their way across the lobby to the front door, but then I can't take it anymore and I rush across the lobby to catch up with them.

"Leave her with me," I shout, but Pedro doesn't stop.

"It's not okay, what you did."

He opens the door to an old-looking car and lets Willow in.

"Pedro, please. I'll phone social services," I call as I run across the parking lot, but he gets in and drives away before I reach them.

"There's nothing we can do right now," Peter says. He's followed me outside, and together we watch the car disappear.

But that can't be the end of it. Not after everything we've been through. If Pedro thinks he's getting away with this, he's got another think coming.

"Yes, there is. I'm phoning social services," I say. "I'll tell them everything I know about him."

Peter nods. "Yes."

"Yes," I say again. Because it's always better to try.

THIRTY-NINE

Ivan

Des has been nice to me for a while. He cooks me food and even finishes the back orders for shelving and a set of stairs I got behind on. Maddie comes in the mornings and sits with me in the front yard and reads me stories, or sometimes she brings her paints. We can hear Des working around back. Bo and Peter come by too. They bring fish. They help Des with the work. And when it turns out that Des has somehow, miraculously, still got his delivery job, Peter tags along to give him company. For a week or two life seems so good. The truth is, my arm is much better. Still broken, of course, but there's no pain anymore, and I could do most things for myself, but I like being waited on.

The only thing that makes it hard is that Pedro and Willow have disappeared.

"It seems they never even went home," she says. Des and I are in the backyard, looking at the specs for a chair a woman in town has ordered. I've never made a chair before, so Des has agreed to help.

"How can a person just disappear?" I ask.

"Somehow, they have," Maddie says. She turns to Des and asks, "Have you heard from him?" Maddie asks Des, but he shakes his head.

"I don't think I'm likely to. He wasn't too happy with me when I made him come back for Willow," Des says.

"You mean the day you left her here alone?"

"I didn't think I'd be gone long."

"Several hours is long," I say.

"You're not going to let me forget that, are you?"

"Why should I?" I say.

He stares at me and Maddie for a second, then throws his goggles to the ground and stomps across the yard and into the house. Like a kid. A fucking kid.

"It's my fault," Maddie says.

"That Des is acting like a kid?"

"No, that Pedro and Willow are gone. I told him I was going to phone social services."

"You think that's why he's gone? So they don't come and get Willow?"

"Yeah, probably," Maddie says. "It makes me so mad to think about it. So mad."

"Yeah. A kid shouldn't have to grow up like that," I say.

"No kidding," Maddie says. She leans over and taps my cast. "No kidding."

* * *

By the time Maddie leaves and I get myself into the house, Des is sitting in the living room watching TV. There are three empty beer bottles beside him, and I know we're starting again. I knew it wouldn't last. It never has.

"Beer?" he says, pointing to the case beside him.

"Thanks," I say. He reaches out to grab me one, but I beat him to it, only I take the whole case.

"Hey!" Des says.

"Enough, Des. Finally, enough."

"What do you mean?"

"I can't live like this anymore. I'm your son, not your caretaker. I shouldn't have to pick up after you. I shouldn't know how to make you throw up."

"I'm only having a few beers," he says.

"That's what you always say, and then you drink so much I end up cleaning up after you."

"You don't have to do anything."

"I shouldn't have to come home every fucking night and check that you haven't lit yourself on fire or choked on your own vomit or left broken bottles lying around where we can step on them. I shouldn't have to do any of that, and I'm not going to anymore."

"What do you mean?" he asks.

Three beers isn't a lot for Des. He's still pretty much with me right now, so it's a good time to say this. "I'm moving out."

He laughs. "You don't have any money or anywhere to go."

"I don't need a lot of money, and I do have somewhere to go. Bo and Peter have offered me their back room until I can find somewhere else. Maybe I'll move to Victoria and get a job. I could probably stay with Maddie's aunt Alex for a bit until I got settled."

"You really want to go?"

"I don't want to, I have to."

Des slumps back into the sofa; his arms droop by his side. "I'm sorry, Ivan. I really am. I tried, you know. I'm so sorry," he says.

It's not what I expect, and it almost makes me change my mind, but what Maddie said is true. If it's not okay for Willow, it's also not okay for me.

"I think you should get help, Des. That doctor guy at the clinic seems nice. Go talk to him."

"And you'll just be at Peter's?"

"For now, yes."

Des stands up and says, "Give me the case. I'll drain them down the sink. I'll change, Ivan, I promise. Starting now."

"It's too late, Des. I've made up my mind."

"You're only eighteen—you can't make this decision for yourself."

"I can and I have," I say.

"I promise to change, I really do."

But I've heard that so many times before, I can't believe it anymore.

"I'll see you soon, Des. I'll just be down the hill. Try not to burn Grandma's house down. I'd appreciate it if you don't do that."

Des has tears in his eyes as he follows me up the stairs and into my bedroom, where I pull the backpack out from under the bed and put my clothes in it.

"I'll come by tomorrow, or maybe I'll send Peter. That'd be better. I'll get Peter to stop by tomorrow and see how you're doing," I say.

Leaving the house with my pack on my back, I feel a hundred feet tall and as tiny as a mouse at the same time. I don't know if I've made the right choice, but I do know I can't keep on going the way I was. Maybe Des will get better, maybe he won't, but I can't keep hiding his problem or making it my own.

I should have done this a long time ago.

FORTY

Maddie

"Come in," says Peter when I knock on the studio door.

I seldom come out here. It's Peter's private domain, and he discourages visitors, but today I have something important to say that can't wait until he comes into the house.

"Look," he says, handing me an almost finished violin.

"Oh, it's beautiful. Where'd the spruce come from?"

"Remember just after the fire there was that barge that went over and lost all those logs? Des salvaged a bunch, and he gave me some. Nice wood. There were a couple of pieces that were dry enough to use right away."

We both study the violin, and I'd bet we also both think about Des.

"What did you come out here for?" Peter asks after a minute.

"Peter…" It's hard to say what I want to say, and holding this beautiful violin in my hand doesn't make it any easier.

He made it for me. For the part of my tuition at Emily Carr that isn't covered by the scholarship. But my mind is made up, and I have to tell him.

Peter reaches out and takes the violin from me. "This violin, Maddie. I made it to sell for your tuition, but I've been thinking a lot about what you said to me and Bo the other day, about how we looked but didn't see. We've done that to you too, haven't we?"

My heart is so full, I can only nod.

"I have a buyer already, you know. He's ordered another one too. So here's the deal. I'm going to sell these violins, and the money I make from them I'll put in an account. If and when you decide to go to Emily Carr, or wherever, the money will be there for you. If you aren't at university, you're on your own, but when you do go, Bo and I will have a little fund waiting for you."

It's more than I hoped for, and all I can say is "Thank you."

As I leave the room, Peter says, "And Maddie, you should get your driver's license. That would be helpful."

"Yeah. I will."

AFTERWORD

Maddie

River, Jack and Noah arrive through the back door, carrying boxes of pizza. They're followed by their sisters and then by Katia, Bea and Sally, who I wasn't expecting but who hugs me close and says, "You should have told us."

We sit in a circle on the floor.

"So what color are you painting it?" Jack holds a slice of pizza up to his mouth and bites, the cheese and tomato oozing out the sides.

"We'll start with white primer. Grab any brush and roller and any can. The whole place needs to be covered. Walls, ceilings, trim, everything."

We're painting Ivan and Des's house. Bo and Peter have taken them to Victoria so Des can check in to some kind of clinic he's found there. I didn't think Ivan should have to go, but apparently the doctor says it's best if the whole family is there to support the person entering the clinic. The whole family means Ivan. And Bo and Peter. I stayed behind to get the house painted, since it looks like Ivan's going to be on his own for a while. He can stay in our back room for a bit, but maybe if the house is nice he might want to come back here. All his tools are here, all his stuff.

I also stayed home in case we hear any news of Willow and Pedro.

Jack shoves the last of his pizza slice into his mouth and picks up a brush and a can of paint. I've already opened and stirred the can, so he only has to dab his brush in and walk to the wall. In big, bold letters he writes *SURF* on the wall, then stands back. River claps. He jumps up and takes the brush from Jack. *SEALS*, he writes, then hands the brush to Noah. *RAVEN*. He hands it to Kyra. *STORM*. She passes it to Laurie. *FUN*. She hands it back to Jack. He puts more paint on the brush and walks to the next wall. *WATER*. He hands it to Bea.

Around and around the walls we go, writing words until the whole space is covered. A wash of white words. Then, when there is hardly any space left, Jack hands the brush one more time to River. *LIVE*. He hands it to Noah. *LIFE*. He hands it to Katia. *LOVE*. She gives it to me. *IVAN*.

ACKNOWLEDGMENTS

Some books take a long time to write, and this is one of them, so I first want to thank Laurie Elmquist, Julie Paul and Alisa Gordaneer for listening to so, so many drafts. Your patience and encouragement mean the world. Thanks also to Joanne Hewko for learning to surf with me; to Dave Pinel and Caroline Fisher for housing me in your lovely camp and sharing the coast with me; to Michelle Mulder, Robin Stevenson, Alex Van Tol, Caleb Schulz and Alexis Martfeld for reading through the jumble of an early draft. Thank you, Sarah Harvey, for your vision. Rowan, thank you for sharing the world you and your friends live in with me, and Michael, thank you for keeping up with the changes over the years, for bringing me hot tea in my sleeping bag on cold coastal mornings, and for always keeping a space for my writing.

KARI JONES is the author of numerous novels for young readers and teens. She lives on the west coast of Canada with her husband and son and their dog, Tintin. For information, visit www.karijones.ca.

MORE GREAT YA...

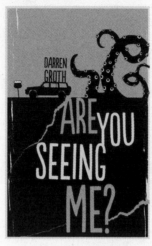

9781459810792 PB

It's been a year since their dad died and Justine became the caregiver for her autistic brother, Perry. Now Perry has been accepted into an assisted-living residence in their home-town, Brisbane, Australia, but before he takes up residence, they're seeking to create the perfect memory by embarking on the road trip of a lifetime in the Pacific Northwest.

For Perry, the trip is a celebration of his favorite things: Ogopogo, Jackie Chan movies and earthquakes. For Justine, it's an opportunity to learn how to let go—of Perry, of her boyfriend, Marc—and to offer their estranged mother the chance to atone for past wrongs.

But the instability that has shaped their lives will not subside, and the seismic event that Perry forewarned threatens to reduce their worlds to rubble...

9781459808164 PB

Harriet (known as Harry) is a donor-conceived child who has never wanted to reach out to her half-siblings or donor—until now. Feeling adrift, Harry tracks down her half-siblings, two of whom are in Seattle, where Harriet lives. The first girl she meets is fifteen-year-old Lucy, an effervescent half-Japanese dancer. Then she meets Meredith, a troubled girl who is always accompanied by her best friend, Alex. Harry and Alex are attracted to each other, but things are complicated by Meredith and secrets Alex is keeping from Harry.

As decisions are made around whether to contact their donor, the three girls negotiate their relationship and Harry tries to figure out what she really wants.

9781459809765 PB

Just when Isabelle thinks her life can't get any worse, something happens to her at school that makes her wonder how she can continue to look after her younger siblings, Evan and Maisie, work at the local mini-mart and deal with her alcoholic mother. It's more than any sixteen-year-old should have to bear, but Isabelle can't think of a way out that won't hurt her brother and sister.

When Isabelle punches a girl at school, only one teacher sees past Isabelle's aggressive behavior. Challenged to participate in a group writing project, Isabelle tentatively connects with a boy named Will and discovers an interest in (and talent for) the only kind of drama she can control—the kind that happens on the page.